THE SPIDER:
CITADEL OF HELL

THE **MASTER** OF **MEN**!

SPIDER®

CITADEL OF HELL

By Grant Stockbridge

ALTUS PRESS • 2019

PUBLISHING HISTORY

"Citadel of Hell" originally appeared in the March, 1934 (Vol. 2, No. 2) issue of *The Spider* magazine. Copyright 2019 by Argosy Communications, Inc. All rights reserved.

CHAPTER 1
THE FLAMING DEATH

A GRAY Packard touring car skated out of Thirty-seventh into Fifth Avenue, tires swishing on the rain-blackened street. It straightened out, its rear swaying wildly, and lunged uptown with motor roaring. A cry rose in Richard Wentworth's throat. He slapped the horn button, wrung a startled squawk from his Hispania Suiza's polite trumpet.

It was a blast of warning, a warning of impending death. How horrible that death would be, even Richard Wentworth did not realize!

He stood on the accelerator, then with a bitter curse, snapped his foot off. This was not his battle. If he blundered into this, he would ruin the whole strategy of his war on the extortionists. His lips twisted into a thin smile as, eyes straining forward over his roadster's gleaming nose, he let his car idle, while ahead the battle lines were drawn.

Fifth Avenue, its street lamps like evil yellow moons, was as deserted as it ever became. Distantly a few taxis prowled. A double-deck bus lumbered downtown.... And ahead four autos maneuvered in a mad game of tag with a human life the prize.

Wentworth caught a gleam of white in the back window of Hanford Tyson's racing limousine, a gleam of white that was the face of a frightened man. Before and behind him, disguised police in two Ford coupés rode guard. As the gray Packard, its

1

speed mounting with each bellowing revolution of its motor, charged down on Tyson's limousine, one of the police Fords spurted to cover the left flank.

The second Ford, riding ahead, braked sharply, dropping back to help in the defense.

Still Wentworth forced himself to idle along. If the extortionists escaped, he would track them to their headquarters—and his lips became a straight hard line—The Spider would

Tyson's car was a torch of roaring fire.

wreak the toll of his justice upon them! His hands clenched tightly on the wheel. It was hard to stay out of the battle....

Guns spat crimson from the two police cars, spewing lead at that charging gray brute of a Packard. Its speed was unchecked. Straight for the nearest Ford it raced. At the last instant, it swerved and slammed into the narrow gap between Ford and limousine. Wentworth saw the police driver deliberately throw his car into the path of the charge, take the full brunt of that

3

smashing, three-ton juggernaut. The crash was like the blast of judgment.

The Ford's shattered nose spun in a mad half circle to the left. Its rear started to follow, slapped the snub nose of the passing double-decker bus. It was like a smack in the face of a drunken man. For a terrible instant, the Ford straightened up. Then its churning wheels flung it, hurdling the curb, completely through the plate glass window of a clothing store. The *papier-mâché* figure of a woman was draped across the hood. The men inside did not move.

These things Wentworth saw in a flash. He saw, too, that the Packard, sheering an instant from that brutal collision, flung on again, shot past the Lincoln limousine. Grimly Wentworth stamped the accelerator. When the police failed…. A missile glinted as it arched from the gray car through the window of Tyson's limousine. Then the Packard was sprinting ahead.

The remaining police Ford roared after it, pistols coughing.

The Lincoln slowed to a stop. Wentworth snubbed brakes to check his mounting speed. That missile! What could it have been? While Wentworth was braking, still a half block away, the street was bathed in red as with blood! The pavement glistened with it. Windows shone with it. Tyson's limousine was a torch of roaring flames!

THE FIRE was inside the tonneau where that missile had been hurled inside where Hanford Tyson sat! Yellow tongues of it, dripping black smoke, flapped as if in fearful mockery from the windows. Within the Lincoln, a man screamed horribly.

Wentworth flung to the pavement, sprinted forward. He saw the man in the back of the limousine on his feet, a black, arm-tossing figure. One more scream started and stopped. Only flames showed now. The heat of them struck Wentworth in the face like a physical blow. He tried to charge nearer, found it hopeless. He checked in his furious race, retreated, slow foot behind slow foot. Yes, it was hopeless. Within that inferno could be only death.

His face twisted by rage at the crass brutality of that murder, Wentworth whirled and flung himself behind the Hispania's wheel, jerked it into swift motion. For an instant, as he lurched forward, searing heat lashed him. Then he was past the burning pyre. The motor's purr deepened to a hum, became a deep throated roar. Ahead, far up the Avenue, Packard and police Ford sped like comets though the darkness. The Hispania's speedometer needle wavered at seventy-two.

As Wentworth flashed past Fifty-Seventh Street, tires shrieked. Ahead the gray Packard rocked and skidded into Central Park. The Ford squealed, locked tires, swung crazily, then rocketed on in its wake.

Wentworth ignored the Park. The Hispania's speedometer read seventy-six as he passed the entrance, scooted northward along Fifth Avenue, paralleling the east drive of Central Park which the killers and police followed.

Wentworth had not acted blindly in choosing Fifth Avenue. He knew the intricacies of the Park as thoroughly as he knew the rest of New York. He knew that presently the Packard would throw off the police and race on to the gang's hide-out, Wentworth was prepared to pick up the trail when the police let go.

Wentworth jerked a sideways' glance, eased his accelerator slightly. He was drawing ahead of the chase. Without warning, his eyes were dazzled again by a lurid burst of fire! He braked, flashed another glance at the Park. The pavement of the east drive behind the Packard burst into flames. Tongues of it leaped twenty feet into the air! Wentworth heard brakes scream.

The police Ford fought frantically to dodge that roaring mass of fire, but the car staggered and swayed into it, burst through with blazing tires and under-structure. The two police piled out, started to stagger away, as the night was torn open by the overwhelming blast of the gasoline tank!

WENTWORTH DUCKED, slammed on the gas, saw a body hurtle through the air. His lips moved in low-voiced curses. Here indeed was work for the Spider.

He was flashing past Ninety-Second now. If the gangster car did not swerve out of the Ninety-Sixth Street exit into Fifth Avenue, the next opportunity to leave the eastward drive in the Park would be a curving crossroad to the west, which would permit an exit at One Hundredth Street on Central Park West.

Wentworth cut gas, braked the Hispania with little stabbing jabs at the pedal. The Packard roared past the Ninety-Sixth Street exit, swept on up the eastward drive. Wentworth spun the Hispania into the Ninety-Seventh Street cut that burrowed beneath the Park roads. In seconds, he had crossed the Park. Braking heavily, he rolled out into the street that bordered its west side—Central Park West. Wentworth rolled north for two blocks, parked just south of the Hundredth Street exit, motor purring.

Tense moments dragged past, with no sign of the gray Packard. Had he miscalculated? Would the gangster car race on northward the whole length of the Park, would it take the southbound drive along the western side of the Park, and double back on its trail? Or would it, as he had deduced, make its exit here?

Abruptly a thin smile twisted Wentworth's mouth. He drew the gear shift back into low, eased the Hispania forward. The killers' gray Packard loafed out into Central Park West and turned north.

CHAPTER 2
A HINT OF HORROR

THE PACKARD was leafing along now, once more a pleasure car. Wentworth, grim-mouthed, paced it at a distance. He was in no hurry. These two would pay later. First the Spider must find the gang's headquarters.

Wentworth's gray-blue eyes, watching the Packard over the sharp, polished nose of his Hispania, were narrowed in thought. His alert, vital face, keen beneath the jaunty brim of a black Borsalillo, was frowning. Hanford Tyson's murder by an incendiary bomb was a new horror added to the arsenal of extortionists. Its fearful torture would persuade future victims not to notify the police, as Hanford Tyson had done.

New to extortionists, yes, but perhaps not entirely new to

outlawry. In his pocket were newspaper clippings of a half dozen incendiary fires in recent weeks, scattered throughout the country. They had been unusual fires, quick-starting, blossoming almost immediately beyond control. Such bombs might have caused them. A swift frown crossed Wentworth's face. Was there a tie-up, he wondered, between these scattered blazes and Tyson's death? With such chemicals as these, houses, factories, entire cities, could be wiped off the earth in a few hours' time!

Wentworth's mind was jerked back to the chase as the Packard he was watching whirled a corner. Wentworth speeded an instant and followed. The killers' car had stopped. Two men alighted. As Wentworth coasted past with muttering motor, they crossed to a smaller car in which two other men sat. It got under way instantly.

Wentworth let them pass, lounging with deceptive carelessness behind the wheel. The chase went on, angled off toward Yonkers.

As they threaded Yonkers' narrow streets, Wentworth, fearing that his pursuit might have been detected, parked his car and grabbed a cab. The trail swung toward the river. Blank-eyed warehouses reared high brick walls on either side. The cab driver cast an uneasy glance over his shoulder.

The car ahead turned to the left, close by the waterfront. Wentworth leaned forward, loosened the left hand door, drew his gun. The cab jounced over rough cobbles, made a second sharp left turn behind the Auburn.

The cab driver jammed on brakes with a startled curse. The Auburn was parked broadside across the street!

AS THE cab shuddered to a halt, two men sprang to its running boards, one on each side, thrusting guns inward at Wentworth.

But it was Wentworth's automatic which spat first. The man on his right arched backward with a hoarse cry and pitched to the cobbles. Wentworth's left foot shot out, caught the door he had loosened and slammed it outward, knocking the second gunman flat. Wentworth dived out upon him.

A roar behind him, dwindling. The taxi driver had jerked his cab backward, whirled out of the street and was gone. Wentworth caught his prisoner by the collar, jerked him to his feet—and from the blackness toward the river, more guns blazed. Lead whined past.

Wentworth ducked, jerking his prisoner between himself and those blazing guns. He heard the pluck of bullets into the man's body. The man cried out and slumped against Wentworth. Wentworth let him fall. He zig-zagged in a crouching run across the street into the shadow of a dark doorway.

No more pistols roared now. There was no sound in the street at all, save the distant clatter of a factory. The deserted Auburn, with its headlights streaming into the blackness, almost filled the narrow thoroughfare. The bodies of the two men lay in the street unmoving. Wentworth slid from the doorway, retreated to the corner, and, running swiftly on his toes, circled toward the river. He peered around the building.

On a railroad siding stood two box cars. Beyond, stretching

out on a wharf to the river, a factory showed lighted windows, the factory whose mechanical clatter he had heard. Wentworth's eyes narrowed, as he identified the place. This was a sugar factory, a refinery operated by the sugar trust of which Hanford Tyson was the head. A freight steamer was moored to the dock beside it, and chimney smoke thrust a black feather against the deep blue sky.

Was it possible that the killers, not content with slaying Tyson, planned to loose their incendiary bombs upon the factory also?

He crowded his wide shoulders into the narrow passageway between the box cars and the factory wall, advanced cautiously.

At the end of the box cars, Wentworth crouched and peered up the street. No one was outlined against the Auburn's lights. From the factory came the louder clatter of machinery. That was the only sound in all this deserted, lonely neighborhood.

Wentworth frowned, stared at the factory. Were the gunmen there? Had they planted incendiary bombs in the building? If they had, scores of lives were in grave peril. The flames from those bombs would envelope the factory within two minutes after they burst.

Wentworth's mouth closed grimly. Keeping to the black shadows, bent almost double, he sprinted toward the factory. AS HE raced forward, guns spoke once more from the blackness behind, pouring out lead that sang viciously after him. Wentworth, with a muffled cry, flung to the ground and lay motionless. Hard-heeled shoes beat a quick retreat. He sprang to his feet, raced the last twenty-five yards to the factory.

There could be no doubt now. The ambush proved that somewhere in the factory were planted incendiary chemicals which would turn it into a living inferno at any moment. He jerked at the factory door, found it locked.

His hand flew to a compact tool kit beneath his arm, drew out a lock pick, and in thirty seconds the door yielded. He slid inside, peering down a dim corridor between offices. Only the upper floors were lighted. Here was darkness.

A red light gleamed at the end of the shadowy hall, walled on each side by opaque glass doors of private offices. Beneath the light Wentworth made out a red fire alarm box. With an exclamation, he darted toward it.

A door flung open to his right. Wentworth jerked up his gun, then hesitated. The hesitation undid him. For into his path a girl sprang, a girl on whose uncovered head gleams of light glinted redly, whose soft young shoulders were hunched forward tensely. And the light glinted on something else. It glinted on metal in her right hand, a gun leveled at Wentworth!

The girl drawled out words, words that were husky with anger.

"I thought you'd be coming here tonight. You tell me where Denny is, or I'll shoot."

Wentworth took a step, nearer her, ready to seize the gun.

11

"Stop," the girl cried hoarsely. "Stop. You've got until I count three...."

CHAPTER 3
DEAD TO THE SPIDER!

WENTWORTH STARED with surprised eyes at the girl, at the pistol leveled at his heart.

"One!" said the girl. She was all but breathless in her tense excitement. Her gun hand was taut and shaking.

"Have you got a permit for that gun?" Wentworth demanded sharply.

He took a slow step toward her. The girl started to jerk the weapon tip, hesitated, and Wentworth seized her wrist, tore the weapon from her hand.

"Now get out of here quick," he snapped. "Wait for me outside. This place is going up in smoke in half a minute!"

The girl wrenched free, plunged toward the hall with its red gleaming fire light. She screamed, once, twice, three times at the top of her lungs. Wentworth cursed, raced after her. At the fire box he smashed the glass with the revolver, jerked down the alarm lever.

Instantly throughout the factory, raucous gongs began to clang. A siren up above somewhere lifted its wailing voice, died, wailed again. The girl darted toward narrow stairs that led upward, stumbled and banged her head against the iron banister, crumpled to the floor.

Wentworth darted to her, dropped the gun into his pocket

and picked her up, his arms beneath her knees and shoulders. She was limp, head lolling backward with hair streaming like fire. He strode toward the exit door, and hard steel jabbed suddenly against his ribs. The girl's eyes were blazing upward into his.

"You're no cop," she said. "Put me down or I'll shoot."

Wentworth strode on. "Listen," he said. "I don't know who you are or what this is all about, but this place will be on fire in seconds. There are bombs here!"

The gun ground painfully into his loin. "That's just another stall," the girl insisted, "put me down, or…."

Wentworth put her down. He did it by letting his arms drop. The girl sat down hard on the floor, a small gasping scream in her throat. Wentworth jerked himself backward and her gun-flame singed his head. The girl yanked the trigger again and again.

The second bullet plucked at Wentworth's coat. He made the cover of the stairs before the third slug whizzed past.

"You killed Denny!" the girl screamed.

Another bullet pinged off the iron railing. Feet clanged on the steps above. The gongs still dinned. The siren wailed. There were shouts, and the fire bombs let go!

ONE INSTANT the hall was shadowed, dimly lit by a red bulb. The next, it was brilliant with fierce red flame. Dozens of the incendiary bombs burst, spattering liquid fire over walls and floor. Lurid spires of it spat to the ceiling, mushroomed. The heat was blistering. The foot steps halted on the stairs, fled back. A door slammed. The girl screamed. There was pain in it.

13

She stumbled down the hall, gun still gripped in her hand, saw Wentworth and threw up the weapon.

"Damn you!" she screeched.

Wentworth sprang forward as she fired, caught a hooked arm about her waist as he darted past and flinging her over his shoulder plunged toward the exit door. That was her last bullet, he knew. The girl beat his back with a fist that clenched the revolver.

Flames stretched out burning, snatching hands at them, flicked a taunting red whip across his legs. His trousers smoldered. Wentworth hit the door at full speed. It slammed open and he took the steps at a single leap. The girl's struggling threw him off balance and they spilled to the muddy earth.

The girl wrenched free, struck at him viciously with the revolver while he struggled to his feet. It glanced across his forehead, ripped the flesh. Wentworth caught her ankle and spilled her flat on her back. Her feet flew high, tossed her skirts into her face. Before she could fight clear of them, Wentworth wrenched the gun away and threw it far out into the black swirling waters of the Hudson. Then he caught her by the arm, jerked her up and away from the factory.

Fire engines were clanging through narrowed streets now. On Wentworth's back, the heat of the blaze was terrific. He jerked a glance over his shoulder. Flames boiled from the two lower floors of the three-story factory. On the upper floor, dozens of white faces showed at the windows, were jerked away. Men shouted and fought. A body tumbled, like a dummy, struck the ground and lay still.

The girl was still fighting, sobbing hysterically. Wentworth thrust her ahead of him as firemen raced past with a hose already stiffening with a high-pressure stream. A crew rushed by with a lifesaving net. A ladder wagon rumbled out onto the wharf, whirled within inches of the black water, its tower already snaking skyward. The river for a hundred yards gleamed as if with infernal light. Factory buildings a hundred feet away had reflected fires in their own windows.

Wentworth thrust on. Blood streamed from his wound, blinding him. He brushed it away with his hand. This girl knew something. From her the Spider might wrest a clue to these demoniac destroyers. He pinioned both her thrashing arms, lifted her again, strode on.

A FIREMAN halted him. "What the hell's this?" he demanded.

"Her boy friend's back there in that," Wentworth said jerkily. "I had to carry her out by force."

"Denny! Denny!" the girl screamed. "You killed him!"

The fireman stepped aside. Wentworth strode on, shoved the girl ahead of him into the narrow passageway between the standing box cars and the factory wall. Lurid shadows danced ahead. What was that! A crouching shadow! A man!

Wentworth dropped the girl, wedged himself between two freight cars. A gun flamed in the dark. Lead gashed the brick of the wall. The girl huddled fearfully on the ground. With frantic speed, Wentworth clawed his way to the car's roof.

In a running crouch, he raced the car's length to the spot below which the gunman crouched. Without a second's pause, he leaped into the crevasse between wall and car. A white face glimmered from the cave of shadows beneath the trucks. A startled oath ripped out. Wentworth ramrodded his fist into the half-seen face. The man snarled in pain, dived out, threw down his revolver.

Wentworth's gun was swifter. It spat upward from his hip. The man's head jerked upward mechanically. He slammed against the box car and went down.

Slowly Wentworth climbed to his feet. He peered along the narrow alleyway against the building, saw the girl pull to her feet. He wiped blood from his face with a fumbling hand, stared down at the man he had killed. He had wanted to capture the man alive, to trace the gang through him, but it had been kill or die.

Back there in the factory, scores of men and women were dying without hope of rescue. Horrid screams of pain rang into the night. A million dollars in sugar and machinery was going up in smoke. Wentworth's worst fears had been realized. Truly, this gang of criminals aimed at more than extortion. Lord! What destruction, what murders threatened! They were using this weapon of hell to destroy property—but what was their purpose? The Spider must learn, and when he did….

Wentworth's mouth was a grim slit. Here was a warning to the gang. From his pocket, he drew a platinum cigarette lighter, its sides glinting with the flickering dance of the fire. He bent over and pressed its base to the dead man's forehead. The shadows were thinner now. The flames must be mounting. As Wentworth straightened, stared, with thin lips twisted, down at the body of the gangster, something on its forehead that was not red.

Wentworth turned toward the girl, then stumbled hurriedly along the wall. She had vanished! Without warning, white light stabbed into his face. He flinched, threw up a protecting arm.

"There he is!" he heard the girl cry shrilly. "There's the man that set the factory on fire!"

"Up with them, punk!" a man ordered harshly. It was a policeman.

Criminals the Spider killed without compunction. They were corruption spreading vermin to be stamped out. But this man represented the law which Wentworth violated only because, sometimes, it aided more than scourged the criminal. Against the police the Spider's swift, deadly guns were useless.

Slowly Wentworth's hands went up.

Another light stabbed at him from behind. A second officer's gruff voice beat through the narrow passage.

"All right, Bill," it called. "I got him, too." Then came a startled curse. "Hell, he killed a guy back here!"

Wentworth stood rigidly with his hands upraised, guns leveled at him from before and behind, guns he could not fight. Blood trickled from the tear on his forehead. He shook his head sharply to spread the flow. It would disguise him, and—God knew, the Spider had need of disguise now. The thin white scar on his right temple began to throb. A pulse in his throat thumped in slow tense beats, waiting for the cry from the policeman behind him.

For that small red spot that had glittered like blood on the forehead of the dead man, the spot that had remained when he had removed his lighter from the face, that spot was a small vermilion seal with sprawling hairy legs, *the seal of the Spider!*

That calling card of death would identify Wentworth as the Spider, wanted for a score of murders. The fact that all his victims had been criminals, slain in the name of justice, did not alter the fact that these killings were crimes in the eyes of the law. For once there seemed no way of escape. A gun before, a gun behind, close walls on either side....

CHAPTER 4
CAPTURED!

ONE THING Wentworth could do. He could attempt to throw the police off guard and that he did. He swayed on his feet. The wound on his forehead was reason enough for that. He pretended faintness and leaned, half limply, against the box car. And he waited—waited for the cry from behind that would brand him as the Spider!

A low startled curse, a man's voice trying hoarsely to articulate. The words when they came were stammered with excitement.

"Mother in Heaven! It's the Spider!"

Words began to pour from the officer, stumbled over each other in the man's eagerness. "Geez, Bill, this here fella that's killed has got the seal of the Spider on his forehead. That means this other guy here is the Spider. Watch him, Bill—for God's sake, watch him! There must be fifty thousand dollars out for his scalp."

The light that glared into Wentworth's eyes wavered. The policeman's hand was trembling.

"Don't come near 'im, Bill," the cop behind Wentworth warned. "You stay there and cover us with the gun. I'll slip the bracelets on him."

"O. K.," drawled Bill. "Listen, guy! One move out of you—just one move, see?—and I shoot."

Wentworth's answer was a groan. He seemed scarcely able to remain on his feet. But in those drooping shoulders his muscles were taut and ready. He heard the mud-sucking feet of the policeman behind him coming cautiously nearer.

The cop behind Wentworth grunted. His fingers bit into Wentworth's shoulder, jerked him about. Wentworth reeled, stumbled as if his feet were clumsy and pitched against the officer. As he reeled, his hand slid into his pocket, jerked out a gun, and jabbed it into the officer's body.

"Follow my orders," Wentworth grated. "And I'll let you live. Pretend to put the bracelet on my wrist. But make one move to lock it, and I'll shoot."

WENTWORTH FELT the officer's body grow rigid, heard breath hiss through his clenched teeth. But no other sound escaped him.

"You all right, Dan?" the officer with the light called anxiously. "Listen, Spider...."

"Say, 'Hold your horses, Bill, I'm O.K.,'" Wentworth whispered. And the officer, parrot like, repeated the words. There was such haste in them that they seemed genuine. Wentworth took the free end of the handcuff in his fist, reeled back against the wall, so that the steel link between them was visible to Bill. "Now help me along," he whispered.

The policeman who supported the stumbling Wentworth, felt the Spider's ready gun rasping his ribs.

Finally, they were clear of the narrow alley. The first policeman, under Wentworth's orders made a pretense of searching his prisoner for weapons. Wentworth flung a swift glance about him. The factory roof had crashed. Walls had crumbled. Nothing but the shell of the sugar refinery remained.

Tito Caliepi

Richard Wentworth

A huddled group of a half dozen men was being treated beside an ambulance. None of the other factory workers was visible. God in heaven, had they all perished? Wentworth was stunned by the enormity of the crime perpetrated by the bombers. And the Spider, would be blamed for it.

He must escape from the police and bend frantic efforts

toward discovering the real criminal. He glanced up the dark streets, still lighted luridly by the leaping flames. Fire trucks were jammed hub to hub. Hoses were coiled and sprawled across the cobbles like lianas in a tropic forest.

A police cordon, men standing almost elbow to elbow against the crowd that packed the street beyond, blocked any possible escape.

Stolidly the policeman whom Wentworth held at gun point plodded toward the line, the other officer marching behind with his gun. The bracelets glinted in the firelight and from the crowd a muttering murmur rose. Police of the cordon twisted their heads, stared back.

"Wait a minute, Dan," called the cop behind. "I don't like the sound of that mob. It might get nasty. S'pose we park right here until the wagon comes."

Wentworth prodded Dan with words. "Say, 'Yeah, I guess you're right.'"

Wentworth was still uncertain in his walk. His head sagging forward. His knees were bent as if he could scarcely keep upon his feet. With a tug on the bracelet, he directed Dan toward a factory door that yawned blackly to their right. The policeman called Bill closed in, shouting, "Get the wagon. We got a suspect." Then his excitement got the better of his caution. *"We got the Spider!"* he shouted.

"The Spider!" The word banged against the imprisoning walls, echoed up the street. The crowd caught it up, and the mutter became a roar—a spontaneous outburst of hatred and rage. Who could expect the crowd to know what the Spider fought for? To the mob he was the supercriminal of the world. His capture at the scene of the fire meant that he was responsible for the many who had died.

The crowd surged against the police lines. A cop fired two shots into the air as a warning. The roar of the mob became louder, filled the street, like the battering of angry seas upon stone. The policeman behind Wentworth came even closer, startled at the result of his thoughtless cry. His face was white. He glanced toward the angry mob in the street.

It was the moment Wentworth had awaited.

He caught the policeman whom he held at gun point, and hurled him against his brother officer. The two men sprawled in a heap. Wentworth darted into the factory doorway. His gun was in his hand. Two swift shots smashed the lock almost at the instant his shoulders struck the door. It flew inward, and he plunged headlong into the darkness.

He heard feet pounding behind him, whirled a corner and almost pitched headlong down ladder-like steps. He crouched low, made the steps in two great bounds. He raced on toward the end of the building where the glass of a window showed gray.

Wentworth leaped to the window, jerked it open. He was behind the crowd. It had broken through the police lines, was charging madly down the street. And once more, he heard that dread, familiar cry, "The Spider! The Spider! Lynch the Spider!"

Wentworth rolled out the window, sprang to his feet, and walked swiftly down the street. When a cop slammed up a window he had turned a corner....

TWENTY MINUTES later Wentworth found the Hispania where he had parked it and shot back toward New York City. Not to his own, but to the apartment of Nita Van Sloan, he sped first. Nita Van Sloan, the one woman in the world he trusted with his secrets, the one woman he loved. He entered furtively by the servants' entrance and elevator, sounded three curt peals on the bell, his signal.

Nita's feet were swift within, her hand was quick on the door. She took one glance at Wentworth's blood-smeared face, his muddied clothing and, with pain tightened mouth, stepped aside.

"Sorry to come this way, beautiful," Wentworth threw at her, striding swiftly toward the bath. "But I couldn't go to my own quarters. I may have been recognized tonight."

A great Dane pranced its bulky body about him like a puppy, blocked his passage.

"Down, Apollo!" Wentworth ordered, and the dog obeyed instantly, tail thumping like a snare drum. Wentworth strode on to the bath.

Before he had sponged clean his face and painted out the forehead wound with materials from his ever-ready makeup kit, Nita had brought some of his clothing which she had insisted on keeping at her apartment for emergencies.

"In my coat pocket, darling," Wentworth told her, studying in a mirror his work on his forehead," are newspaper clippings. They'll give you some idea what we're up against this time. Wholesale arson! And I want you to make a phone call!"

He gave her instructions and closed the door. He dressed

swiftly, strode out to find Nita garbed in a trim blue street suit, with a close black straw drawn jauntily down upon her gleaming chestnut curls. The yellowed newspaper clippings were in her hand.

The beginnings of a smile curved the red of her lips, but she shook her head sharply. "Dick, don't you see what this means?" she demanded, holding out the clippings. "They're *destroying food*. Everyone of these clippings tells about burning a warehouse or a factory that has to do with food. And tonight it was Hanford Tyson, head of the sugar trust."

Wentworth nodded slowly, eyes keen upon her face. "And tonight in Yonkers," he told her softly, "they destroyed Tyson's sugar refinery!"

"Then, you knew!" Nita cried.

"I read it that way, dearest," he agreed. "All these fires seemed incendiary. Only something as deadly and swift as those bombs used tonight could have spread the flames the same way in each case. There's no doubt about it. Some fiend is destroying the country's food supply!"

Nita's voice was hushed with dread. "Surely, surely, in this time of want," she said, "no man could do a thing like that! It would be inhuman."

Wentworth's alert, vital face was grim, the line of his jaw lean and hard. Once more, he knew, the Spider was at grips with one of those master criminals whose warped and ruthless brain, whose ghastly plots blanched the face of the world with their incredible cruelty.

He took Nita's arm. "Come, dear, I can see you are determined to go with me. There can be but one reason behind this destruction of food," he went on as he whirled the Hispania swiftly toward police headquarters. "Money is at the root of every major crime. Some man, or some syndicate, wishes to raise the price of food to terrific heights by the destruction of competitors' supplies. The fact that thousands may starve does not matter, if only the food destroyers fatten their private pocketbooks...."

THE COMMISSIONER of Police, Stanley Kirkpatrick, rose gravely to meet them. It was two o'clock in the morning, but with such a crime as Hanford Tyson's death to be solved, even four or five o'clock would find him still at his desk.

"They caught me at the theatre," said Kirkpatrick, in explanation of his immaculate Tuxedo. "I understand you were on the scene when poor Tyson was killed."

Wentworth jerked his head in a nod. "I came to ask if you minded my working on the case, and to ask you to help me. Nita insisted on coming along."

Kirkpatrick bowed to her slowly. "If I could always count on such inspiration, that chap, the Spider, wouldn't beat me to the kill so often."

Nita's smile was easy, her blue eyes as gay as if she had no idea that Kirkpatrick was thrusting delicately at Wentworth, toward whom suspicion had often pointed.

A slight buzz at Kirkpatrick's phone interrupted her reply. The commissioner's gravity increased as he listened.

He said, "Very well, I shall be here," and hung up, looking directly at Wentworth.

"I have no objections to your working on the case, Dick," he said quickly, "but be careful. I am about to be superseded. Glastonbury...."

Wentworth's eyes narrowed slightly. "Ah, the district attorney." He was silent for a moment. "However," he said swiftly, "that will not prevent your doing something to help, if you will. Here's a list of names, men I'd like to have called into a conference so that I could see them. Most of them wouldn't recognize my name and heed my request, but I assure you...."

Kirkpatrick glanced up from a swift survey of the list. "They're all food men," he said slowly.

Wentworth nodded, tossed to the desk the packet of newspaper clippings Nita had read. "Yes," he said. "Don't you realize that the destruction of the Yonkers refinery was the real object of tonight's attack?"

"But why?" Kirkpatrick demanded frowning. "Surely not for insurance."

Wentworth shook his head sharply. "They did it to destroy food! Perhaps they're taking a tip from the farmers' strike to boost prices."

"You're joking, of course."

Wentworth's face was deadly serious. His eyes gleamed. "I'm not joking. Don't you realize the millions that could be made on a restricted market, by destroying your *competitor's* supplies?" He slapped the desk. "And, Lord! Think of the suffering. Not only those that burn to death, but the thousands whose slim purses can't pay the high prices. Why, man alive, it means famine!"

"**THEN YOU** were at the Yonkers fire?" Kirkpatrick said.

Wentworth straightened, continuing to meet his eyes. He laughed shortly. "You change the subject rather abruptly."

He thought swiftly. It was apparent there was some motive behind the questioning. Kirkpatrick never asked for purposeless information. Had his car been seen near the factory fire in Yonkers? Had he himself been identified despite the welter of blood that had masked his features? There was no way of knowing.

"I followed the men who killed Tyson all the way to Yonkers," he said slowly. "But they lost me there. I knew I was near Tyson's refinery and on a hunch went to it. It caught on fire. It seems fairly clear that the same gang that killed Tyson destroyed his refinery. How many of those poor devils died?"

Kirkpatrick's mouth was a tight line, its corners depressed. "Fifty-three."

Wentworth's face went white. "Good Lord! Fifty-three, in addition to Tyson and your three men in one night. Fifty-seven murders! Kirkpatrick, we must stop these arsonists. Will you call that meeting?"

Kirkpatrick looked down at the list in his hand. He nodded his head heavily. "Your theory is fantastic as hell," he said, "but it's possible." His eyes met Wentworth's again.

Wentworth's expression did not change. But his pulses hammered a little faster. What was it Kirkpatrick knew? What had happened that brought these repeated warnings from his friend? Was it possible the police who had taken him prisoner knew his identity?

Never before had Wentworth, unmasked and undisguised,

been captured on the scene of the Spider's kill. His own blood had blurred his features, but the glaring white light of the police torch had played upon it—and the police are trained observers.

Wentworth heard the door open behind him. Kirkpatrick's eyes jerked to it, and Wentworth, watching him, knew suddenly that here was the danger that his friend had warned him against. He turned slowly, caught a glimpse of Nita's intent blue eyes, switching from him to the doorway.

In the doorway, a policeman stepped aside and a girl entered, a girl with fiery red hair, the girl with whom Wentworth had grappled in the doomed factory!

Her blue eyes were fixed hatefully on his face. He read in them that she recognized Richard Wentworth as the Spider!

And over her shoulder glared the hostile, small eyes of District Attorney Glastonbury!

CHAPTER 5
A TELL-TALE WOUND

IT WAS plain that the girl was ready to accuse him of having been in the factory just before the fire broke out, that she would identify him as the man whose seal upon the forehead of a dead man had aroused the cry of "*The Spider!*"

It was plain, too, that Glastonbury, his keen, long-nosed face thrust forward pugnaciously, was ready for that charge and would press it to the bitter end. This, then, was why Kirkpatrick had warned him.

Glastonbury strode past the girl with jerky, bouncing steps, an alert, small man. He knocked the door shut behind him.

Wentworth bowed to him ceremoniously. "Congratulations, Mr. District Attorney. While I've been running in circles, you've really accomplished something."

Glastonbury's small eyes snapped. "What do you mean?"

Wentworth had the best of all possible faces for defense. His was no expressionless poker face. He took refuge in mobility, in creating false expression. Now his face mirrored surprise, raised brows, widened eyes:

"Why, this girl," Wentworth turned and glanced quickly at her, his back to Glastonbury and Kirkpatrick, "this girl is one of the incendiarists."

A startled cry was wrung from the girl. "That's not true," she gasped out. Her high heels tapped across the floor to Glastonbury's side. Blue eyes, bright in a white face, flashed from Glastonbury to Kirkpatrick, to Wentworth.

Wentworth waved a cigarette. Smoke curled from it. "Well, perhaps, I'm being swayed by circumstances," he said. "But just after the fire broke out, I saw you run from the factory with a gun in your hand."

The girl's mouth opened in a gasp. Wentworth gave her no opportunity to parry his attack. "What were you doing in that building with a gun?" he demanded.

"Just a minute," Glastonbury bit out. "This girl came voluntarily to me with an offer to identify a man who burst into the factory, fought with her, and carried her captive from the build-

His forehead struck against the corner of a steel filing cabinet and he sprawled limply to the floor.

ing. This man was later attacked, killed his attacker and printed the seal of the Spider on his forehead."

"So that's her story?" asked Wentworth softly.

"Yes," cried the girl, "yes! And it's the truth. And you—you are the man who did that. You set the building on fire. You are the Spider!"

Wentworth lifted his brows in mild amusement, snubbed his cigarette butt in an ash tray. He waved a hand in a resigned gesture, turned to Nita, who, watching intently, had kept carefully in the background. "Dear," said Wentworth, "this threatens to be long and tiresome. Don't you want to get to sleep? If you'll phone Ram Singh, he'll drive you home…."

"Look here, Wentworth…" Glastonbury broke in.

Wentworth swung toward him with elevated brows. "I was speaking to the lady," he said, and turned back to Nita.

"Thank you, Dick, I would like to," she said. "Call me in the morning."

Wentworth escorted her to the door. "Good night, Stanley," she called to Kirkpatrick, and was gone.

GLASTONBURY POUNDED across the room, jabbed a stubby finger against Wentworth's chest. "Don't think you can bluff me, Wentworth," he bit out, "or stall me by being high-hat. This girl has identified you…."

The girl took a stride nearer Wentworth, her eyes glaring hatred.

"You know you're lying," she panted. "You know that you came into the factory and did what I said you did. Why, I—I hit you over the head with a gun. I—"

"Did you really?" said Wentworth. He touched the top of his head with exploring fingers. "Strange that I should forget. And I assure you I have a very good mind for pretty faces, and—" he looked her over admiring, "figures."

The girl stamped her foot. "Oh," she cried, "Oh, you're impossible."

Wentworth's mouth twisted in a slight smile. The girl stood staring at him with angry eyes. Abruptly, she sprang forward and struck at Wentworth's forehead with her fist, catching him a painful blow upon the painted over wound her gun had made.

Wentworth fended her off with an indignant arm.

"Restrain yourself, my dear," he said calmly. "Attacking me won't get you out of a jam."

The girl leaned back against Kirkpatrick's desk, panting. She whirled toward Glastonbury with an outstretched, pleading hand.

"Can't you see," she besought him. "Can't you see that this is only a trick of this man to escape suspicion? I tell you he is the Spider. Ask him how it happened that he was at the scene of the fire. He admits seeing me there."

Kirkpatrick was eyeing her gravely. "I know why Mr. Wentworth was there," he broke in quietly. "Mr. Wentworth is a criminal investigator in an amateur way and frequently assists me on important cases. He followed the murderers of Mr. Tyson to the vicinity of the factory, lost them and ran up to the factory, just in time to see the fire. He was telling me about it before you came in."

"A likely lie," Glastonbury sneered.

"But why," cried the girl, "why would I go to Mr. Glastonbury with my information if I had been guilty of anything? I had a right to be in the factory—"

"Yes, in the day time," Wentworth cut in.

"But I had work to do," the girl cried, insistent. "I was there working—"

"Or were you," Wentworth asked softly, "waiting for Denny?"

The girl's body grew rigid. She jerked about toward Wentworth. "What do you know about Denny?" she demanded.

Wentworth smiled quietly, took one of his privately blended cigarettes from their platinum case. He looked up at the girl, putting flame to his cigarette.

"Quite a lot," said Wentworth, inhaling smoke. "I know quite a lot about Denny. His name is Dennis Carter. He is, or was, an assistant cashier in Mr. Tyson's Yonkers plant. He is—or was—your affianced, or should I say, 'boy friend,' Janice?"

"I knew you were mixed up with that gang of criminals," the girl cried. "I knew it." She took a quick step toward him, seized Wentworth by the lapels. "Where is he?" she cried, "where is he?"

Wentworth shook his head slowly, then detached the girl's hands from his lapels and stepped back. It wouldn't do to allow the girl too close a scrutiny of the clever job of painting that he had done over the wound on his forehead. His eyes were coldly narrowed on hers now.

"What gang are you talking about?" he demanded sharply.

THE GIRL'S head began to jerk from side to side. She retreated, a slow step at a time. "No, no" she cried, "I don't know anything. I don't know anything. All I know is that Denny is gone. Denny, Denny—"

It was as if the name had undammed a flood of words. They poured from her. "We wanted to get married, and Denny told me that some man at the factory offered him some money to do some secret thing, night before last. I begged Denny not to do it. He said he wouldn't. But yesterday, he didn't come to the office and I haven't seen him again. I know he's dead—I know those men who set the place afire tonight killed him. But that's all. As God is in Heaven, that's all."

"Who was that man?" Wentworth demanded. "Who approached Denny?"

The girl rolled her head miserably again. "I don't know. I don't know. Denny wouldn't tell me. I was waiting there tonight, hoping I could find out who at the factory had paid Denny money—hoping that I could force him to tell me where Denny was."

"And you came in," she cried. "You came in. And I tried to shoot you. And after I'd emptied the gun, I hit you there—there on the forehead."

Wentworth shrugged and turned away from her, walked toward Kirkpatrick and Glastonbury. "It looks as if," he said, "we might get a clue to this gang lay tracing the movements of Dennis Carter."

Glastonbury's glare was hostile. Kirkpatrick was staring at him fixedly. "Yes, it does," he admitted. "Where did you find out about this Denny Carter?"

"I called up Tyson's secretary," said Wentworth shortly. "Asked about a redheaded girl employed at the Yonkers plant, got her name and some other stuff about her, including the information about Carter."

"I see," said Kirkpatrick. His eyes were still intently on Wentworth's face. Glastonbury made a spring to the police commissioner's desk, twitched up the green shade of the lamp. The dazzling white glare struck full in Wentworth's face. He blinked his eyes, threw his hand up to shield them and to keep the light from falling directly upon the painted-over wound upon his forehead. He was expert at such matters as that painting, but doubted that even his skill could escape detection in that vivid light.

"Take down your hand," Gastonbury bellowed. "You're hiding the wound on your forehead! You painted it over!

Wentworth stared fixedly into Glastonbury's glittering dark gaze. Would his work stand the inspection of these sharp eyes beneath the glaring light? If the paint showed even a suspicious shininess, Glastonbury would be within his rights in demanding that Wentworth submit to an examination which nothing could escape. If that wound upon his forehead were disclosed, then all the girl's story immediately became substantiate; then he became the man who had killed a gunman and stamped him with the Spider's seal; then Richard Wentworth was identified as the Spider!

WENTWORTH FELT a high heavy beating of his heart. He felt fear, cold in the pit of his stomach. Not fear for himself— Wentworth had played the game too long for that—but fear for the thousands who must die at the hands of these arsonists, unless the Spider tracked them to their hideout, struck like a God of destroying anger among them. He must remain free.

"Wentworth," bit out Glastonbury, "take your hand away and let me see your face."

Wentworth stiffened with apparent indignation. He threw back his head. The shadows from his brows, thrown upward by the glare of the light, obscured his forehead. He jerked his hand to his side, turned away from Glastonbury.

"Kirkpatrick," he said vehemently, "I've stood quite enough of this suspicion. I've tolerated it previously because Glastonbury is, in a sense, your guest. But it's gone quite far enough. Good morning." He pivoted about, starting for the door.

"Stop!" Glastonbury ordered. A thin smile twisted Wentworth's mouth. He had not expected that Glastonbury would let him get away with that. It was too simple a trick.

Wentworth took another stride. His feet seemed to become entangled. He tripped, half recovered, stumbled and plunged headlong. His forehead struck against the corner of a steel filing cabinet violently and he sprawled limply on the floor.

A CRY wrenched from Kirkpatrick. He circled the desk in two strides, sprang to Wentworth's side. Glastonbury and the girl stood rigidly, staring with wide eyes. Kirkpatrick caught up his friend's body, rolled it over. There was a stain of blood upon the floor. Across his forehead, where the sharp edge of the metal had cut, there was a bloody wound from which crimson drops oozed slowly.

Kirkpatrick's voice roared out. "Garrity, quick! Get the surgeon. Bring water." The door slammed open. A policeman's carroty red head thrust in, took in the scene with wide eyes. Then the head was jerked back. Kirkpatrick sprang to a water cooler in the corner. He doused his handkerchief, crossed rapidly back to Wentworth's side and began to bathe his temples.

"Dick, old man," he said. "Are you hurt badly? Dick," he called insistently, "Dick!"

Glastonbury pounded over and glared down at him. "Damned clever," he snapped.

Wentworth blinked up at him. "What happened?" he muttered.

"You tripped over your own feet," Kirkpatrick explained, glaring up at Glastonbury, "fell and banged your head against the cabinet."

"Baloney!" sneered Glastonbury, "he pretended to trip and slammed his head against the cabinet to keep us from proving he'd painted out the wound."

Wentworth raised a hand slowly to his forehead, looked at his fingers stained with blood.

"You won't get away with it!" Glastonbury hammered on.

"Oh, shut up," said Wentworth wearily. He struggled to his feet with Kirkpatrick's help.

"Keep quiet a moment, can't you, Glastonbury?" Kirkpatrick jerked out.

But the District Attorney was at their heels, yapping his anger like a crotchety lap dog. Wentworth sank into Kirkpatrick's chair, took the stained handkerchief his friend had used to sponge his temples and, despite the pain, mopped the wound with hard-pressing fingers.

If the surgeon was coming, he would have to remove the last traces of paint from his forehead now, lest it be detected. He peered about the room and abruptly dropped his hand from his forehead.

"Where's the girl?" he asked sharply. Glastonbury whirled, stared about, strode to the door.

Men raced away, searching, but they came back empty-handed.

The girl had vanished.

A faint smile chased itself across Wentworth's lips. "Your witness seems a bit bashful," he told Glastonbury. "Or perhaps she was afraid that we might find out the true reason for her being in the factory."

The doctor strode in, a brisk man, with eyes that perpetually squinted as if from too much peering into a microscope. He dressed Wentworth's wound deftly, and Wentworth was glad to lean back in his chair. His head throbbed painfully.

He closed his eyes, but the rasping of Glastonbury's voice jerked them open.

"Doc," the district attorney demanded, "are there any traces of paint on that wound?"

Wentworth, peering upward, saw that the doctor did not lift his face. "Nope," the medical man said.

"Isn't that wound," Glastonbury persisted, "an old one re-opened?"

"No way of telling that," the doctor said, as he continued to work.

Wentworth heard Glastonbury rasp out a curse. "You won't

get away with it, Wentworth," he snapped out. "Kirkpatrick, I want four men."

Kirkpatrick's voice, answering, was grave and slow. "What for?"

"I am arresting Wentworth." Glastonbury pounded out words like bullets. "I'm going to put him where he can't escape. In Sing Sing under guard."

"We have a jail here," Kirkpatrick protested.

"Yes," Glastonbury agreed, and sarcasm sharpened his voice, "and Wentworth has escaped from it. I have the governor's permission to use Sing Sing." He paused. His words became slow, ominous. "I get the four men, Kirkpatrick?"

"Of course," Kirkpatrick agreed, and left the room. The doctor completed the cleansing of the wound, taped gauze across it and left. Wentworth sat slowly erect, leaned upon the desk and smiled slightly, as he lit a cigarette.

"What's the charge, Glastonbury?" he asked quietly.

Glastonbury strode portentously to the opposite side of the desk. He thrust a finger at him like a weapon. "You, Richard Wentworth, are the Spider!" he thundered. "I have a warrant

Xavier Jones

J.J. Callahan

JANICE HALLY

Glastonbury

Smail Perkins

for your arrest for homicide. You have used your red seal of death once too often."

CHAPTER 6
NITA TO THE RESCUE

G LASTONBURY'S DRAMATIC charge did not alter the careless smile upon Wentworth's face. He blew out smoke casually.

"You don't say," he remarked. "And may I ask who is charging me with homicide?"

"I am," Glastonbury thundered.

Wentworth raised his brows. "Richard Glastonbury, Commonwealth's attorney in and for the county of New York, upon his oath of office, doth depose that to the best of his knowledge and belief, that the said Richard Wentworth—what's the rest of it, Glastonbury? Whom am I accused of murdering?"

Glastonbury grinned at him, lips lifting from glistening teeth. "At least twenty men, Mr. Spider."

"Only twenty!" Wentworth murmured. "But surely you're not naming all of them in that little affidavit of yours."

"No," said Glastonbury "No!" He took another pace nearer Wentworth and shook a stubby forefinger in his prisoner's face. "I am charging you with the murder of—Hanford Tyson!"

Wentworth smiled pleasantly. That smile came from the depths of him. Tyson! Good Lord, of all the men he had killed in his crusades of justice, of all the men he had stamped with the little red calling card of death, his Spider's seal, Glastonbury picked Tyson, a man he had not killed—a man who had not even worn the seal!

Glastonbury saw the genuineness of the smile and sneered at him, an angry light in his disagreeable, small eyes. "Think it's easy to beat, eh, Wentworth? Then listen to this: A police officer can swear that you trailed Hanford Tyson's car from his home to the spot where he was killed. Furthermore, you covered the retreat of the car which hurled the incendiary bomb. Three police can swear to that. Furthermore, I have an affidavit from a responsible source that you were on the scene when the Yonkers fire broke out, a fire which was identical in every way with that which killed Tyson. And don't think, Mr. Wentworth, that you'll get out on bail. This is once when your money and your name will do you no good."

Kirkpatrick strode back with four police. Glastonbury snapped at them. "Draw your guns and guard that man," he ordered.

Wentworth was still smiling. He had not realized that the man could throw together such a damaging case. It was circumstantial, but the things the man said were true. At least the case would be strong enough to throw him into jail, and that he could not permit.

This gang of fire murderers was undoubtedly plotting now the destruction of huge quantities of food. They sought solely their personal profit. They had no thought for the thousands their man-created famine would strike; they cared nothing for the fact that the people of the nation, just struggling upward from the depths of the depression, were barely able to stretch meager pay into a livelihood.

Wentworth knew these things, but he had no proof of them. To others it was just a wild theory. But he knew its truth with fearful certainty. Not for his own sake, but for the sake of suffering, imperiled humanity, the Spider must be free to battle the Destroyers, the bringers of famine!

He threw a casual, veiled glance about the room. Four guns leveled on him from as many different directions by four police. Not a chance to run for it. No chance, either, to persuade Glastonbury he was wrong, or—failing in that—to persuade him it was more important that Wentworth remain free than that the supposed murderer of Hanford Tyson go to jail.

"Watch him, men," cried Glastonbury. "If he makes a break for it, kill him!"

WENTWORTH TURNED his back on the man's glower of utter rage, smiled pleasantly at the detectives who crouched with a desperate tension behind their leveled guns. "Let's get going," Wentworth said. "I have a luncheon engagement and, after all, it takes a certain amount of time to wangle a *habeas corpus* out of these judges."

"Put handcuffs on him," Glastonbury barked. "Put them on his ankles, too."

Wentworth stood calmly and submitted to the shackles. He turned and smiled wryly at Kirkpatrick. "Don't forget that meeting," he said. "It's even more important now. You can see Glastonbury won't listen to my theory."

"Your theory? Bah!" exploded Glastonbury.

The police caught Wentworth by the shoulders and hustled him forward, his ankles jerking painfully against the short chain that held his feet together. Wentworth stopped abruptly, ducked forward at the waist and the two men shot past him.

"Hold him," Glastonbury shouted. "Shoot him if he runs!"

But Wentworth made no attempt to run. He faced toward Kirkpatrick and bowed suavely with an apologetic smile.

"Good morning, Stanley," he said.

In the squad car a man sat on each side of him. A third sat on the front seat beside the driver and another swung onto the running board. And they all held their guns ready. Glastonbury trailed in another car.

Without permitting himself to be observed, Wentworth studied the positions of the detectives. The man on his left had his gun in his left hand, held awkwardly. Obviously he was right-handed. The man ahead was twisted about, his gun resting on the back of the seat. The man on his right and the one on the running board had their weapons leveled too. Four guns.

Wentworth knew he could free himself of the handcuffs by an old Houdini trick, a sliver of steel which he always carried would do the trick, thrust beneath the ratchet and dog that locked the cuffs upon his wrist. His ankles could be similarly freed, but not while the guards watched him. Wentworth went to work at once.

A car swerved into the street ahead of them. "Keep clear, there," the guard on the running board warned.

The auto's siren ripped out a whining wail. The man in the front seat twisted about, stared at the car. And Wentworth, too, watched secretly.

The driver was dark-skinned, with a cap drawn down over

his eyes. In the back, behind drawn curtains, another figure showed dimly. The driver jerked his head toward the police and poured out a mouthful of gibberish.

Then the small, closed car sprinted ahead, jerked to the middle of the street, fairly in the path of the police, and squealed to a halt. The driver sprang out on the far side and fled in a zig-zag run. Hoarse yells burst from the cops.

"It's a trick! Watch him!"

Without warning, flames burst out in the car ahead. They billowed from open windows, and a man's black figure was outlined against their dancing red!

"It's another murder!" the cop on the running board yelled hoarsely.

Springing to the ground, he dashed toward the stalled car. **THE GUARD** on the front seat snarled, "Watch him," over his shoulder and sprang to help.

The guard at Wentworth's right leaned forward over his gun, staring at the flames, which by this time had enveloped the entire car.

Wentworth's left hand struck with dazzling speed, snatched the gun from the man on his left. In the same instant his fist flashed across and slammed against the man's chin. The guard slumped limply. The detective on his right cursed, jerked up his gun. But Wentworth's captured weapon slashed in a glinting arc. It caught the guard between the eyes and laid him unconscious in his corner.

The driver gasped out an oath, snatched for a weapon. But Wentworth jabbed his captured pistol beneath the man's ear.

"Get going," he rasped, "and get going fast." For an instant the man hesitated. Then, as Glastonbury shouting excitedly from the car behind, came near, he slammed into gear and shot the squad car forward.

"The first corner to the left," Wentworth ordered. They burst by the blazing sedan, and the guards whirled with startled shouts. They threw up their weapons, and hesitated. Their own companions were in the fleeing car. They could not fire.

For five twisting blocks, Wentworth fled in the police machine. Then he ordered the driver to stop the car and, snatching a second weapon from the floor, he climbed out.

"Get going," he commanded, "and keep going. If you even slow up, I'm going to empty both of these guns into the car. I don't think all of the bullets could miss you. Turn the second corner to the right."

He stepped back, weapons leveled. The driver threw a single frightened glance over his shoulder and clashed gears in his anxiety to get under way. He spun away up the street. Wentworth stooped, pressed the muzzle of the gun against the anklet chain and fired twice. The chain snapped. Then he raced at top speed around the corner into an alleyway.

A coupé was parked there. Wentworth sprang into it and instantly it lurched forward, spun out of the alley and loitered off into crosstown traffic. Wentworth turned gravely to the girl at the wheel.

"Thanks, Nita," he said quietly. "That was a tight spot."

The girl flashed blue eyes at him. "Ram Singh got away all right?"

Wentworth nodded. "That cap changed him completely. And when he started spitting Hindustani to tell me what to do, I could hardly believe my ears. The police thought they were being cursed with words they couldn't understand, and it had them tied in knots."

The smile that touched Nita's red lips was very faint indeed.

"When you said to phone Ram Singh, I knew you meant trouble threatened. And I knew if Glastonbury arrested you, he wouldn't keep you in Stanley's jail. Ram Sing and I planted a dummy in the back of that sedan Ram Singh drove and doused the whole car with gasoline. We waited and saw you come out handcuffed."

"A damn smart trick, darling," Wentworth told her. He placed his hand upon her arm. For a moment she jerked her eyes away from the traffic to stare deeply into his. Their smiles said more than any words.

Her voice grew brisk. "Your kit of tools is in the pocket of the car. There's a suitcase in the back with some clothing, money and guns."

Wentworth nodded. "You're right. I'll have to disappear. I won't communicate with you, except through Ram Singh until I've beaten this murder rap. Glastonbury outlined a rather formidable circumstantial case against me, and I know the man well enough to realize that he must have an ace or two up his sleeve, in addition to that. I won't tell you where I'm going to be. I don't know. It will be better that way."

As he spoke, Wentworth dipped into the pocket of the car, took out a compact kit of chrome steel tools and from it, drew a lock pick with which he speedily removed hand and ankle cuffs.

"The next corner, darling. Stop there and I'll be gone."

"But, Dick," protested Nita. "You've got no hat, and with that bandaged head somebody will be sure to spot you."

Wentworth smiled at her, repeated, "The next corner, darling."

"Dick, you must let me hear from you, you must."

Wentworth nodded grimly. "Right, and in the meantime, see what you can do toward getting this Janice Hally to withdraw the affidavit she gave Glastonbury which identifies me as having been in the factory before the fire was started. This case will require all my ability. I don't want to spend most of my time dodging Glastonbury."

Nita slowed the car reluctantly. Wentworth threw an arm about her. For an instant their lips met, then he was out, had grabbed the suitcase from the back of the car and was striding off up the street, conspicuous with his hatless, bandaged head.

WENTWORTH FOUND a furnished room for rent and paid a week's lodging in advance. Five minutes sufficed for him to change his clothing. Rapidly then he went to work on a disguise and, at the end of ten minutes more, stared at himself fixedly in the mirror. Long black hair, parted in the middle, fell below his ears. His skin was sallow, and his nose was long and pointed. As he stared at himself, Wentworth bent slowly forward, stooping his broad, muscular shoulders and hunching one so that the smooth fit of the black tweeds to which he had changed was completely disarranged. He was an emaciated, hunchbacked man now, with the anemic face and the quick, frightened eyes of a cripple.

He pulled a large black felt down over his hair, threw a cape about his shoulders, and, picking up his suitcase, left. A half dozen blocks away he rented another room. He gave the name of Tito Caliepi, left his suitcase there and went to a nearby drugstore where there was a public dial telephone. He knew that a call from such an instrument could not be traced—and from it he phoned Kirkpatrick.

"Stanley," he said, when the police commissioner's precise but slightly wearied tones came over the wire, "you know by this time that I found it inconvenient to remain in Gastonbury's hands and so eluded him. I just wanted to request that you go ahead with that meeting of the food magnates. I'll get Nita to attend and be my eyes."

"I'm going ahead with the meeting," said Kirkpatrick grimly, "for my own information. It's obvious Glastonbury will spend the rest of his time running you to earth, and I'll have to catch the arsonists."

"The food destroyers, Stanley!" Wentworth corrected. "When and where is the meeting?"

"Nita will go as my guest," Kirkpatrick said steadily. "And I warn you, her phone wire will be tapped. I've been ordered to capture you, and the entire machinery of the police department will be devoted to that task."

Wentworth laughed, said "Thanks for the warning," and left the booth swiftly, a hobbling, bent old man.

Back in his crowded little room, a few hours sleep served to refresh him. After which, altering his disguise, he went to the street again.

He made two phone calls and found out that one Smail Perkins was at his home on upper Fifth Avenue. He went there. But it was not the hunchbacked old violinist now who sent up his name to Smail Perkins, of the Produce Exchange. It was a young clerk who carried a heavy leather brief case. He went up twenty floors in a silent elevator, crossed a hall and was admitted by a grave butler. Smail Perkins, a tall, thin man with nervous hands, received him alone in his library.

Wentworth bowed awkwardly from the doorway.

"Well, what is it? What is it?" Perkins jerked from behind his desk.

Wentworth muttered sounds, stepped forward and abruptly thrust a pistol beneath Perkins' nose.

"Come with me," he ordered.

Perkins reeled to his feet, walked ahead of Wentworth from the room, received his hat without a word from his butler and stumbled out into the hallway. Wentworth placed him in a taxi, drove to his room, and tied him to the bed. He extracted the information that the meeting had been called by Kirkpatrick for three o'clock in the afternoon at the offices of the Tyson Sugar Corporation in the Sky Building.

Then, gagging Perkins, Wentworth proceeded to don the man's clothing and with putty and paint made his face over into the thin jawed likeness of Perkins. In this disguise, he checked all his belongings at a hotel, and presented himself punctually at the offices of the Tyson Corporation and was admitted to the directors' room where Kirkpatrick sat gravely at the head of a long table with Nita at his right. At his left sat Glastonbury, his face in belligerent mold.

WENTWORTH'S ENTRANCE seemed to be a signal to Kirkpatrick. He rose slowly. "All you gentlemen know of the death of Hanford Tyson last night and the destruction of his Yonkers plant," he said. "The newspapers all carry this as the vengeance of extortionists. I want to tell you that these threats of extortionists are simply a blind, that the real purpose of these fires and murder is the control and destruction of foodstuffs with the purpose of establishing a monopoly and utilizing it to boost prices out of all reason.

"I called you gentlemen together because you represent practically every major branch of food supplies and their distribution."

He produced Wentworth's clippings, read the accounts of fire after fire that had destroyed food stuffs.

Callahan, head of a meat packing firm; Xavier Jones of Amalgamated Can; a dozen others pooh-poohed the entire thing as ridiculous. They said they had received no threats, and Glastonbury capped the climax by saying he refused to believe it; that the whole thing was just a trick of the Spider, to hide the extortion plot by which he chose to enrich himself.

Wentworth felt his face grow grim. As usual, no one would believe until it was too late. As usual the Spider must battle alone against the Underworld. And the danger of attending this meeting had gone for nothing. He had hoped....

Xavier Jones rose heavily from his chair, a tall, thin man with sunken jaws that looked as if he had lost his molars and not replaced them.

"I would feel gratified," he said with a voice as sepulchral as his appearance, "if I could accept what you say. I have been threatened, and I am very much afraid that the attack is upon myself instead of my holdings. I ask you, Mr. Police Commissioner, to keep this secret. I prefer to guard myself."

Wentworth's eyes went to him quickly, studying the man. Here at least was some hope, a lead he might develop. But he had no opportunity to question Jones about the matter, for Kirkpatrick, after offering his help and being refused, closed the meeting and turned to Nita. And Jones left before Wentworth had an opportunity to approach him.

He waited until he was certain Kirkpatrick was back at his office, then phoned him in mockingly disguised tones and told him where Smail Perkins would be found. He waited until night, recovered the things he had checked and rented new quarters, then hurriedly made himself up as the old hunchbacked violinist again.

He entered a subway station, sped uptown, and went on to the vicinity of the Park Avenue home of Xavier Jones.

Wentworth gained entrance to the building through the tradesman's door, dodged the hall boy and made a slow climb up many flights of stairs to the top floor. Jones' terrace was on the west. The east apartment was vacant. Wentworth's lock pick opened the door of the vacant apartment in a few moments' time. He eased in, straightened with a gasp.

The white gleam of a flashlight struck him in the face.

"Lift those hands, guy!" a high excited voice demanded. "What the hell are you doing here?"

There was tension, shrillness in those tones. Wentworth knew them. They were the tones of a man half-crazed with dope. In the back gleam of the flashlight, he could see a leveled gun that trembled.

"Hold that gun steady," he ordered calmly.

"Who the hell do you think you're giving orders too?" the voice went on shrilly.

There was a mounting hysteria in the words, and Wentworth knew that death leered at him from the shadows. A gun in the hands of such a man was a death warrant for anyone who crossed his fantastically inflated ego.

"Who are you talking to?" the man raged on. "By God, I'll show you—you can't talk to me like that."

The gun jutted forward, trembling but pointed very accurately at Wentworth's body.

"I'll show you," the man whimpered, and scarlet flame lanced from the muzzle of his gun.

CHAPTER 7
FANGS OF THE SPIDER

WENTWORTH'S DODGE to one side and forward as the gunman shot was lightning swift. The split-second warning that the man intended to fire was all he needed. A second shot scorched past his face. Then he had wrenched the gun away and a short, powerful blow had sent the man reeling back. His light flashing wildly about the room, went out in a crash of glass.

Wentworth's own light stabbed through the darkness, picked up the man stretched senseless on the floor, then flicked over the room. It was empty of furniture. There was little doubt that the soundproof walls would have smothered the pistol shots.

Wentworth crossed back to the man, stooped and slapped him twice heavily in the face. His eyelids twitched open. He stared wildly into the dazzling white of the electric torch beam.

His voice rambled: "I never meant no harm. I was just lookin' for a place to sleep."

Wentworth thrust his face forward until the reflection of the light showed his long-nosed, made-up profile, showed the straggling long hair, drooping on each side. It was not a pleasant face. The eyes burned into those of the prostrate man.

And staring into that face, the man at last was silent. His eyes ceased their restless roving, became fixed and somewhat glassy.

"God, don't look at me like that," he moaned.

"You're going to answer some questions," Wentworth said quietly. "You're going to tell me why you are here. You are going to tell me what you were planning to do."

The man's voice died to a whimpering moan. "I can't. I can't!"

"Did you ever hear," asked Wentworth softly, "of the Spider?" THE GUNMAN'S eyes stared fascinatedly into Wentworth's. "Yes," he whispered. "Yes!"

"I am the Spider!" Wentworth allowed his thin lips to part into a smile that was horrible to see. And the man on the floor screamed. For he saw white teeth and the canines on either side were long and pointed. Wentworth had fitted celluloid points over his own teeth.

"Those," said Wentworth, "are the fangs of the Spider. You wouldn't force me to use them, would you?" He leaned even closer to the man, baring those pointed white teeth again. "Talk, fool!"

"Oh, God," moaned the man. "Keep the Spider away."

"Why are you here tonight?"

"I came to throw something into the house of the guy who lives next door."

"Xavier Jones?"

"Yeah, that's him."

Wentworth's eyes gleamed. "Where is the thing that you were to throw?"

"Over in the corner."

"And then what?"

"Then I was to run like hell. Go downtown and help some other bozos throw some more of the things."

The calm monotone, his gleaming eyes, had a hypnotic effect upon the distraught dope addict he held prisoner. "Where are you going to throw them?"

"Down on the East side. Down near Beekman where the boats come in."

Wentworth heard a sound behind him, switched off the light and darted across the room toward where the man had pointed.

His prisoner screamed. "Don't leave me in the dark. The spiders! The spiders! The little red spiders!"

The door thrust open. Wentworth, groping in the dark, found a small glass cylinder that was cold to his hand. He moved on softly, toward double windows that opened on the terrace.

"Halt!" a gruff voice commanded.

"Oh, God," cried the man on the floor. Wentworth could tell by his voice that he had not moved.

White light stabbed out from the door, located the gunman. "What the hell!"

Wentworth's groping hand found the latch of the window, eased it open. He threw open the window, cleared the sill in a single leap and was hidden in the darkness of the terrace. He saw light probe into the night beside him, heard a gun crack, and the bullet sing off into the night.

"The Red Mask!" the dope addict screamed. "The Red Mask!"

WENTWORTH DARTED away from the fire escape, back toward the penthouse, keeping far to one side where the stabbing rays of that white light could not reach. He found the brick wall of the penthouse, crept nearer the window.

Without warning, light streamed along the side of the wall, outlined Wentworth's crouching figure.

"Stay like that," a harsh voice grated at him.

Wentworth had a gun in a hand masked beneath his flapping cape. He could shoot out that light, shoot the man behind it, but he wanted to see, to know what this new terror of the dope addict was, this Red Mask. He stayed "like that."

"Now walk toward me, and walk slowly!" the voice commanded. It was oddly muffled, Wentworth noticed. He shuffled toward the light, his hunched shoulder lifted high, his whole figure twisted and distorted; his head thrust forward beneath the broad brimmed black hat. On he shambled, while the white light held dead in his blinking eyes—on until he was within ten feet, just out of springing distance.

"Halt!" said the voice, and now in the reflected glow of the torch thrown back by the panes of the French doors, Wentworth could make out the man behind the light, big and wide-shouldered.

His head seemed awkward, seemed to perch atop a thick, abnormal neck which grew straight out of the shoulders. And then Wentworth saw the reason. The man had on a hood that covered his entire head, a Red Mask that was like the black hood the executioner puts on a man he is about to hang.

"So this," the muffled voice was sneering, "is the famous Spider?"

Wentworth did not answer.

"Come inside," the voice ordered, and slowly Wentworth obeyed. As he stepped in the door, men seized him from each side, wrested the gun from his grasp. Wentworth made no resistance. He allowed himself to be propelled across the room, thrust against the wall. Then lights went on, and he beheld five men in red hoods and two others who wore black. It was the two in black hoods who stood now with leveled guns while the men in red hoods stood in a line with folded arms and stared at him through narrow slits that shadowed their eyes.

One of the men stood a little forward of the other four.

"The Spider," he said, and once more his words were a sneer.

"The great avenger! The mysterious Nemesis of criminals! And he falls for an obvious trap like this!"

CHAPTER 8
BATTLE IN THE DARK

A TRAP, the Red Mask called it. Wentworth thought swiftly. Had he really walked into a snare set for him by this hooded band? It seemed unlikely, unless the threat to Jones had been made so that he would tell of it at the meeting of the food men called by Kirkpatrick; unless the criminals had known in advance that the Spider would be informed of what went on at that session, and had expected him to follow the trail so established. Wentworth shook his head slowly, and shaking it, smiled, so that the long savage teeth of celluloid showed. He heard the gasp of in-drawn breath that followed, saw the two men in the black hoods shrink back.

No, this was no trap, else the men ready to seize him would have been an overwhelming force, not a single dope addict who fired wildly into the darkness, not a man who would divulge the plans of the arsonists. Abruptly Wentworth darted a look about the room. The dope addict was gone! That meant the fire at Beekman Street was scheduled to start soon. He must get away! The Spider must sound the alarm!

He jerked his eyes back to the red-masked five.

"Just a cheap show-off!" the man with the rasping voice jeered again. "Those teeth are a little absurd. What are they, celluloid?"

Wentworth formed a laugh low in his throat. It was at once

guttural and sibilant. It was not loud, yet it penetrated to the farthest point of the room. He enunciated slowly and the words fairly hissed from his unmoving lips. "They are," he said, *"the fangs of the Spider!"*

The two men in black shrank back still farther. Wentworth thrust forward his head. The white, unshaded light from the ceiling made his sallow skin glisten, threw the beak-like nose into sharp relief. In the shadow of his hat's brim, his eyes seemed to burn and those teeth, those white fang-like teeth… Wentworth bared them with a thin-lipped, evil grin.

A Black Hood threw up his gun with a high-pitched laugh.

"Stop it, fool!" the Red Mask ordered.

The gun leveled shakily, the finger tightened. The Red Mask sprang forward. The other Black Mask swung his head to watch the gun arm struck down.

With another shrill laugh, Wentworth darted forward. His hand brushed the light switch, and the scene blacked out like magic. As Wentworth leaped, he snatched the celluloid teeth from his mouth and grabbing for the gun of one of the Black Masks, he gouged the hand with the teeth.

The man's scream, high and wavering, tore out. *"God! He bit me!"* But the gun skated across the floor.

Wentworth jerked away from him, crossed the room in two great bounds and crouched. Feet stampeded back and forth.

"No lights!" rasped out the voice Wentworth knew. "He's got a gun now. Cover the windows, the doors."

"He bit me, he bit me!" wailed the man.

A sound of a sodden blow, a soft thump of a body thudding

60

to the floor and that voice was silent. All was silence in the room. Wentworth waited, a thin smile playing across his mouth.

He took off his hat, held it before his face so that the sound he uttered would be diffused, so that the guns of the waiting Red Masks could not locate him, and laughed.

TWO MEN let out strangled cries. "Good Lord! Where is he?"

"For God's sake, turn on the lights," another gasped. "I can't stand this."

"Fools!" rasped the leader. "Shut your mouths. Do you want your voices identified?"

Wentworth raised his brows in the dark. So these were voices he could recognize. Or was it simply that the leader feared they might be that? No way of telling. But he could delay his escape no longer. Wentworth straightened and, stepping without sound, strode straight out from the wall.

A hand with a gun jabbed his ribs. Wentworth seized it in both of his, twisted. A man cried out. The gun came loose in his hand. Wentworth reversed it and fired point blank. The man's cry became a scream. As he fell, Wentworth, bent almost double, sprang across the room. He collided with another man, and fired again.

"Get out of here!" The leader rasped sharply. He was moving as he cried, moving erratically so that Wentworth dared not waste one of his two remaining shots on him. "Out before he kills us all. He can shoot!"

Wentworth pivoted slowly toward where he judged the door to be, but he had been whirling about. He was not sure. Move-

61

ment was all about him. Once he leveled his weapon, but the sound at which he aimed faded into nothingness. A door opened. Wentworth spun in that direction, but no lighter oblong showed where it was.

The fangs of the Spider! At last he had buried them in the bodies of these murderers. But it was scant vengeance for the fifty-seven dead in one night by their hell-fire. And tonight flames would sweep another part of the city, unless the Spider....

The sound of another door opening whirled Wentworth square about. He flashed a shot into the darkness. No spear of flame answered it.

If only he dared switch on the light, if only he had guns with full chambers. But he must hold himself in check. If he knew this was the entire organization of the Food Destroyers here, the Spider would be justified in risking his life in a single desperate effort to wipe them out. But he did not know. It was doubtful if so small a group could be the whole of a criminal band which struck far and wide over the country. And only the Spider knew what threatened; only he might check these criminals.

Abruptly Wentworth tensed into rigid listening. More feet were whispering in the room now. Had the whole flight been a pretense? Were they bringing up more forces to capture and eliminate the Spider? Wentworth felt behind him, grasped the knob of a door and opened it soundlessly. He wormed through the opening.

"Lights!" a voice rasped in the room he had quitted.

Wentworth pulled the door shut just in time. A ray of light

stabbed beneath it. He whirled. He was in a kitchen. With a single bound, he crossed the room to a dumbwaiter, jerked it open. Feet pounded now in the room he had left.

"The roof!" the grating voice ordered "Search the apartment. Shoot on sight!"

WENTWORTH STRADDLED into the dumbwaiter shaft, caught hold of the central rope with one hand and let the door click shut just as someone burst into the kitchen with heavy feet. With his free hand, Wentworth manipulated the rope that would lower him. The gun, with one bullet in the chamber, was ready between his teeth, his eyes watched above him.

Down five floors he went until, listening at another entrance to the shaft, he could hear no sound. He climbed out then, slid silently through a dark apartment and found a phone. He called police, cried excitedly that a murder was being committed on the east terrace and gave the address. Then he darted back to the dumbwaiter and completed his escape, slipping out through the tradesman's entrance before the first distant moan of the police sirens quavered through the night.

He moved off down the street, a queer, hunch-shouldered figure in a black cloak with a black hat that hid his eyes. His pace was awkward, but swift. There was no time to be lost. The fire fiends were once more loosing their fury upon the city at Beekman Street, where the boats come in. Tenement houses crowded close against South Street there; congested tenements with rusty disused fire escapes, death traps for the close packed humanity that called them home. The wind was from the east and strong with the breath of March. Once fire seized upon these wharfs, those flimsy tenements, there would be no checking it. Wentworth ducked into a subway entrance, found a phone booth and called Kirkpatrick.

At the commissioner's precise answer: "Kirkpatrick speaking," Wentworth laughed. He made his voice flat and mocking. "The Spider speaking. Tonight the Flame Men strike on South Street. Strike at the wharfs at Beekman. Be prepared, Mr. Commissioner."

"But what wharfs?" Kirkpatrick snapped. "When?"

"Hurry," said Wentworth, still in the same sinister monotone. "Hurry!" And he laughed.

He hung up, but he did not wait for a train. Kirkpatrick would put a tracer on that call and rush his radio cars to the spot.

Reaching the street, Wentworth hurried eastward, climbed to an elevated station, and hunched into a car seat, his hands clasped beneath his bowed chin. He sat, the picture of patience, inwardly seething to be at grips with the Flame Men, while the elevated clanged and clashed its slow, noisy way downtown.

CHAPTER 9
THE FOOD DESTROYERS

THE ELEVATED train was unbelievably slow. It clanked to a stop, the doors banged open, sighed, shut. With a dull clang of bells and the train jerked into a crawl again. Wentworth, madly impatient to be at grips with the Destroyers, sat stolidly with eyes half-closed beneath the down-drooping brim of his black hat.

The train clanked on, and finally Wentworth limped belatedly out the closing door, thumbed down wooden, then steel stairs to the street and raced along Beekman toward the waterfront.

Now that the clatter of the elevated was stilled he could make out the clanging of fire bells, the subdued wailing of sirens. Autos with headlights like bloodshot eyes swung into the street. Still the flames had not sprung up. Wentworth began to hope his warning had been in time, that Kirkpatrick had been able to avert the new attack of the Flame Men.

He made out now a cordon of blue coated police along South Street, blocking off the wharfs. Wentworth slid into a black doorway and cast a swift glance down the broad waterfront. No movement except the police, no sign of skulking figures that might be bombers. Directly ahead were the docks and offices of the South American Steamship Company, specializing in the East coast trade… food imports from Brazil and Argentina. Wentworth frowned, gray-blue eyes intent. Had bombs already been set with a time device? He shook his head sharply. The dope addict had said he was to assist in *throwing* bombs.

Wentworth whirled and raced silently up unlighted stairs. Dim light from behind threw his grotesque shadow ahead of him like some monstrous bat with the flapping long cloak. He pivoted around the banister post at the top of the first flight, sped down the hall, caught the railing again. He used the outthrust arm as a brake, flung himself to the floor.

Gun flame speared at him from above. Wentworth crowded against the railing, waiting, pistol in hand. Luckily the captured gun had proved to be the same calibre as his own. It was fully loaded now. Out in the street, police whistles got excited. Above stairs a man cursed, and there was the sudden sound of a blow, followed by more curses. Wentworth smiled grimly. Someone was paying for the stupidity of that shot. He had been right then. Obviously, blocked from reaching the ship, the fire bombers would take their position on a roof and either throw or catapult bombs to the docks. That had been Wentworth's deduction that had sent him racing up black stairs. The pistol shot confirmed it.

He crawled back down the hall, straightened and clasped the banister, the gun between his teeth. Police feet were racing upstairs. He hoisted himself upward, a few inches at a time. The stair well was wide. Hand above hand, he inched toward the upper floor.

Slowly then, keen eyes piercing the darkness, he flexed his arms until he could peer along the floor of the top story. He spotted a nearby glimmer of white that was a man's face. The face let out a startled exclamation. Wentworth dropped from sight, hung with one hand, snatched the gun from his teeth.

Feet slapped away in panic haste, glass smashed. Instantly the hall was alive with flames that ran and leaped and danced in evil glee. A narrow, spreading tower licked up toward Wentworth. Police shouted raucously two floors down. Their guns crashed, and lead plucked at Wentworth's flowing cloak.

He muscled himself up, threw his body over the railing. He

was up instantly and running in the wake of the bomb thrower. A gray oblong of sky showed an open roof scuttle. A spring into the air, and Wentworth seized its edge and drew himself up to sprawl flat on the roof. He shot a swift glance about, over the neighboring buildings. No movement there.

Springing to his feet, he crossed two houses in a crouching run, pausing to shoot a swift pencil of light from his hand torch over the scuttles. Neither had been opened. Abruptly he whirled toward the river, cursing. A tower of flame thrust a red spearhead into the black night. Other aspiring tongues flapped up to challenge its solitary glory, merged with it and became a vast writhing spire!

THE ROOFS were brightly lighted now. Twenty feet from Wentworth a scuttle burst open, and a uniform cap thrust out into the lurid darkness. A gun glinted and cracked. Wentworth flopped behind a chimney. Gravel cut his palms. Lead chiseled into the bricks, whined off into the night.

"I've got him," the cop sang out. "I'll hold him behind the chimney. Get into the next building."

Wentworth's teeth bared in a smile that was not pleasant. Once more the police were chasing the wrong man, while the criminals got away. He pulled from his pocket the glass fire bomb he had seized from the dope addict. The roof was fireproofed and it could do no serious damage. He tossed it to fall between him and the cop. There came a tinkle of glass, an upleaping burst of flame. The policeman's pistol filled the night with futile sound.

"Stop him, stop him!" a voice howled hoarsely. "He threw a bomb!"

Wentworth sprinted from behind the chimney, not to the next house, but past the fire-dazzled policeman, back to the house where he first had spotted the bomb throwers.

He peered down through the scuttle. The upper hall was in flames, but he saw no one moving in the bright red light of the fire. Swiftly Wentworth extracted from his kit the powerful silk line he was never without. He slipped it, doubled, through a hinge of the scuttle and, shielding his face in his cloak, let himself down swiftly past the licking tongues of fire. Heavy gloves, about which he twisted the line, protected his hands.

The heat was terrific. Wentworth's cloak smoldered. At the second floor, Wentworth hooked himself to the railing with his foot, climbed clear of flame and hauled the line after him.

He fled to the back of the house, peered out. Firemen were hacking through a fence, but had not yet penetrated to the back yard. Wentworth hung at arm's length from the sill, let himself drop. He struck heavily, lost his balance and spilled to the ground.

"There he is! There goes the firebug!" a fireman yelped.

Wentworth hand-vaulted a fence, missed a barrel of ashes by a hand breadth. With a short laugh, he ripped off his cloak and draped it about the barrel, clapped his hat on top of it and, vaulting the next fence, ducked into a cellar window.

A shout from the roof and a fusillade of bullets made him laugh silently.

"I got him!" a voice on the roof shouted.

"Sure," Wentworth grinned to himself. "You got me, just like you got the crooks that set this fire."

HE RANGED forward through the cellar, found a pile of coal, then a grating that opened in black shadow. He made his hands grimy with coal dust, smeared his face and climbed to the sidewalk. He walked directly, openly, toward the police lines! His hands were out-thrust before him, blindly. He stumbled. Strong hands gripped his arms. "Here, what are you doing inside the lines?"

Wentworth winced beneath the grip of those hands. "Cripes! Don't!" he pleaded. "I'm burnt!"

The cops jerked their hands away.

"Where's the doctor?" Wentworth implored. "I was asleep and fire comes running under the door. I try to get out...."

Wentworth was led to a line of people beside an ambulance waiting to be treated. He stood at the end of it. The cop walked away. Wentworth moved stealthily toward shadows, away from the line. A renewed shout behind him! A policeman ran out of a tenement doorway, waving a long black coat and black hat.

"The firebug got away!" he yelled.

The police who had passed Wentworth whirled toward the ambulance, saw him drifting off into the flame-dancing darkness. They drew guns.

"Halt!"

Wentworth ducked behind the ambulance, gained a nearby doorway in three swift strides. He plunged through the building, over a fence, through another tenement to a parallel street, circled back toward the flaming wharfs. Danger and death stalked him there, but… the Spider still had no clue to the identity of the Flame Men and until he did, he would not leave.

From the shadows, he surveyed South Street. A blazing ship had been cut loose and towed out into midstream. The wharfs were doomed. Flames wrapped them like a blanket. Tenements across wide South Street had caught in a half dozen places. Fire equipment was bunched in a messy tangle. Hose sprawled everywhere. Dense smoke, stinking of burning foodstuffs and creosoted wood, rolled like poison gas through the streets, driven on by the prodding east wind.

Everywhere people fled the flames, children and women scuttling with sheet wrapped bundles along the streets. Women and men screamed from windows for rescue while flames ate toward them. Two tenements were already black shells.

Wentworth saw the street wall of one crack, bulge a little. Four firemen were working beneath it, pouring water into the ruin. Wentworth shouted a warning, raced toward them. His cry was lost in the turmoil of cracking fire, gushing hose and bellowed orders. He charged through police lines, wrested a hose from two men and turned its stream on the four firemen. It bowled them off: their feet, rolling them like pebbles on a beach.

The two hose men pounced on Wentworth, snatching at the hose. Then, with the rumbling thunder of an avalanche, the wall collapsed. It seemed to subside rather than topple and spread flying bricks and debris out over the walk, thrust like an over-whelming juggernaut into the street. But the four firemen were clear.

The two hose men stood transfixed, staring with open mouths. Wentworth dropped the hose, darted away again. His face was a grim mask. Four lives saved. But for everyone he snatched from the path of disaster, a dozen would die in this hell-spread fire. And the damage and death was only the beginning.

Tomorrow when the newspapers blazoned the destruction of food, when another and another blaze wiped out supplies, panic would come. Rising prices and meager pocketbooks! Want and famine would stalk the streets, and violence would follow… all this, so that a few soulless men might fatten their pocketbooks. WENTWORTH RANGED over the fire area. The flames seemed to be spreading more rapidly than even the east wind and flying brands could contrive.

Wentworth quested farther westward. Two huge warehouses, storage places of food, were wrapped in flame. A five story tenement wore a girdle of fire at its third floor. On its fourth a woman screamed, holding out a child. Firemen were below with a life-saving net. Wentworth hastened toward them, stared up.

"The crazy fool won't jump!" a net man growled. "I'll go for a ladder."

He lopped off in heavy boots. The other net men stared up helplessly.

"A ladder will be too late," one muttered. He megaphoned his hands. "Jump! We'll catch you!"

The woman screamed meaningless sounds, ducked inside, came back to the window with two children in her arms. She stood there, pouring panic noise into the night. A tongue of flame licked up toward her.

Wentworth scanned the building. The fireman was right. A ladder would be too late. Before it could come, the roof would collapse. Wentworth spotted at a corner, near no windows, a drain pipe that ran upward. Fire did not touch it anywhere. He sprang toward it, looping his silken cord as he ran. Tying a bunch of keys to it, he climbed swiftly up the pipe, gripping it alternately with knees and hands. Dimly, through the deep-throated growl of the fire, he caught the encouraging shouts of the firemen. He climbed on....

The pipe was a torment to his hands. The wind sent hot smoke, a taunting lick of flame toward him. A shout of fear from the street below. He hung on grimly, fought upward. His hands ached with strain, burned with the torture of hot metal.

The third floor windows crawled past. Smoke thickened, billowing upward. He squinted through it. He was level with the woman's window, but ten feet from it. Ten feet of blank wall a cat could not cross. Clinging with one hand and his knees, Wentworth threw the looped, weighted, silken cord upward. The heat-wind from the flames tossed it, whipped it about. It missed. Painfully Wentworth pulled the cord in again.

The ache numbed his arms. He could not feel the heat of the pipe. His knees were rubbed raw against the bricks. He coiled the rope awkwardly. His grip weakened, he felt himself sway outward.

Once more now he threw the silken cord, weighted with the keys, upward. A draft caught and swirled it. It soared on, slapped the blind on the fifth floor window. Wentworth looped the cord, twitching it sideways. The loop caught. It held! Heart pounding, Wentworth wrapped the cord about his leg and swung free of the pipe.

OUT OVER the fiery void he swayed, one hand stretched out ahead of him to grasp the sill where the woman stood. He whirled, erratically, passed the window with his back to it. He set his lips grimly, choking back a curse, kicked the wall to steady himself. Black smoke belched hotly about him. Flames snatched at him. The backswing started. Wentworth snatched at the sill. His fingernails scraped it. Then hands closed upon his, dragged him in close. He threw his other arm inside and dragged himself upward.

The woman stared at him unseeingly. Her mouth was open. The end of a scream was still in her throat. A white-faced boy of twelve still gripped Wentworth's hand, steadying him.

"Thanks," Wentworth muttered.

The woman flung herself upon Wentworth, wrapping both arms about his neck. He thrust her backward, snatching up the first of the children, a baby of two, jumped to the window.

The firemen below let out a shout, held the net ready. Carefully Wentworth tossed the child. It did a slow somersault, and a thin scream whipped from its mouth by the wind of its fall. It struck fairly and bounced into the arms of a waiting man. Wentworth whirled back into the room, threw out a boy of four. He groped through the smoke, found the older boy, half-conscious on the floor. He tossed him out, too.

The mother he found reeling dizzily against a wall. She stared about wildly, saw that her children were gone and charged Wentworth with a scream. He ducked under her clawing hands, caught her by the waist, and propelled her through the window. He sprang instantly to the sill himself. The firemen caught the woman, cleared the net, and Wentworth did a swan dive outward. He ducked his head and rolled, slapping the net with his back.

He sprang out. Men were about him, clapping him on the back. A warning shout rang in his ears. He was jerked violently forward and seconds later a hot gush of air and flying debris slewed out over the spot where he had stood. The roof had fallen in. Bells clanged. A ladder wagon clattered up. Firemen stared upward at the gaping window with their lolling tongues of flame.

Wentworth ducked away from the back-patters. There still was work to be done.

He saw a plume of smoke drift upward from another red brick warehouse, plunged toward it on a dead run. He was stumbling with fatigue. His eyes bleary from smoke, his lungs tortured by it. His head felt numb. He caught at a heavy sliding door. It was locked. He picked up a brick, smashed at it. His first blow missed entirely and Wentworth almost fell. He leaned against the door, panting. He straightened, tried again. The lock broke and he threw his weight against the door. He could scarcely move it.

He strained at it desperately. Hell, he was getting weak as a woman. That climb up the wall had been strenuous, but.... The door began to move. He got it open far enough to wriggle inside and peered about. A furtive shadow, running, caught his eye. He snatched out his gun and fired, thought he saw the figure fall. He stumbled through half-darkness toward the spot. His flash light was gone now. Flames were in the warehouse, but they were at the far end. Their light confused the shadows.

Wentworth broke into a heavy run, pistol ready. Abruptly the floor rose and smacked him in the face. He heard a man curse, felt a shattering blow that seemed to split his skull wide open. He lay still, on his face, with outflung arms.

The figure of a man crouched over him, cursing. He rose, shot a furtive glance about. In all the warehouse nothing moved except the fire-agitated shadows. The man chuckled hoarsely, leaned over and tucked a fire bomb inside Wentworth's shirt, tossed others against the stacks of boxes on all sides. The flames burst out furiously, eagerly. The man slunk off into the shadows.

A door creaked distantly, then all was silent—silent except for the hungry crackling of the mounting flames, twisting and whirling in a dance of death.

Wentworth lay motionless on his face.

CHAPTER 10
OUT OF THE FRYING PAN—

THERE WAS hunger in the crackling of the flames. They devoured boxes, flirted trailing yellow skirts toward the helpless man on the floor. They threw slender arms high into the darkness toward the gabled roof. Smoke played about the fire like a courting male, swirling away from a flick of red, crowding back again as the flames turned to their business of destruction. Food, precious food, became charred and noisome ash.

And the Spider lay helpless, face down upon the floor.

Beside him towered stacked boxes of canned goods. Incendiary chemicals had spilled over them and, red and yellow, the shawl of fire wrapped them. They sputtered and sizzled. A can popped and spewed steaming juice in a thin stream. A fusillade of minor explosions followed.

The warehouse was choked with smoke now. It roamed into remotest corners. It thrust up to the rafters and hung there like a great black bird of evil. It lifted once, settled again. A door had opened, and a draft had quiv-

The fireman threw Wentworth's body to his shoulder, caught the boy and plunged through a hell of smoke and flame.

76

ered through fire and smoke. The flames leaped up more fierce-
ly. The tower of boxes beside Wentworth was seething with
violent reds and whites. More cans burst. The pile leaned dan-
gerously. In a few moments it would topple, spill its mass of
white hot metal and flaming wood upon the prostrate, helpless
man.

Through the murk near the doorway there was movement.
A tall man in a fireman's hat and dripping coat advanced with
a boy who pointed and strained out into the midst of all that
heat and terror. His childish treble penetrated through the
sullen anger of the holocaust.

"But I saw him come in here, and he hasn't come out."

The fireman's gruff rumble was not distinguishable, but he
ducked his head into the heat and thrust on.

"No," the boy protested, "I won't go back. You might miss
him."

The two figures, the heavy, helmeted fireman and the slight,
frail boy, pushed on through smoke and flame. The tower of
destruction beside Wentworth creaked. It sagged on one side,
leaned toward him. Abruptly the boy darted away from the
fireman and, arm before his face, rushed through the circle of
flame that surrounded Wentworth.

He seized him by a foot and dragged, failed to move the
unconscious man. The flaming pile of boxes swayed. Sparks flew
upward. Another dozen cans split and spat out scalding juices.
The boy braced his back, heaved again. Wentworth's body slipped
an inch.

Behind the boy, in the distance, the fireman groped.

"Hello!" he shouted. "Where are you?"

The boy twisted a white, freckled face upon his shoulder, called shrilly. The fireman swung uncertain eyes about, stumbled on through the smoke.

"Hurry! Hurry!" the boy cried. "I've found him, but I can't...."

The tower began to crumple. It did it majestically, like a ship plunging to its last grave. As if it knew the destruction it would wreak by that collapse; as if it were a sentient, evil thing in league with the forces of destruction that had struck here tonight; as if it knew that killing the Spider was a momentous thing to be done deliberately and with ceremony.

Its angle increased. A few inches more and it would topple off balance, make the final fatal plunge.

THE BOY screamed shrilly. He tugged at Wentworth's feet, failed to move him. He caught up a small box and, thrusting it before him like a ram, charged into that toppling pyre. Spears of flame lanced out at him, reached behind the shield. He screamed with its torture but pressed on. He checked the tower's wavering for a moment and in that second of time, while the tower threatened to deluge boy and man in burning death, the fireman burst through the final fringe of smoke and flame.

He caught Wentworth by the feet and hauled him to safety, snatched the boy clear. The tower collapsed. Splashes of fire spurted in all directions. Flaming brands flung wide. The fireman knocked one aside with a coated forearm. He threw Wentworth's body to his shoulder, caught the boy by the arm and plunged back through the smoke and intolerable heat.

Reinforcements had come now. A silver bolt of water shot

from a hose, spattered with a sound like a gigantic frying of bacon over the warehouse inferno.

Outside the fireman laid Wentworth upon the ground. The boy crouched beside him.

"That was brave of you, sonny," the fireman told him while he sought for Wentworth's injuries.

The boy shrugged. "He saved mom and me and the kids," he said. "Climbed up the side of the building and tossed us into a net when we was too scared to jump. I just paid him back."

The fireman jerked erect from his examination of Wentworth. In his hand was a glass cylinder that had come from within Wentworth's shirt where the Food Destroyer had placed it.

"You're talking about some other guy," he said slowly. He spotted a battalion chief and shouted to him. The chief came running. "Some other guy," the fireman told the boy. "This bozo is one of the fire bombers." He held out the cylinder for the boy to see. "This is what they set the fires with."

The boy stood up slowly. He was all of twelve years old. Freckles were rusty polka dots over his white face. His blonde, tumbled hair, singed now from flames, was straggling on his neck. His arms and legs were thin from hunger long drawn out.

"You're lying!" he shrilled into the face of the fireman, his fists balled bonily at his sides. "You're lying! He didn't throw them bombs."

The battalion chief rushed up. "What bombs?" he demanded.

The fireman held it out. "I found this in this guy's shirt after

I hauled him out of that warehouse yonder. Looks like he was trapped throwing bombs."

The kid thrust in between the two men, staring up into their faces, first at one, then at the other. His eyes were strained wide.

"He was not, either!" he shouted. His voice rose stridently. "He did not throw them bombs. He saved mom and me and the kids I tell you!"

The battalion chief stared down at the boy, looked questioningly at the fireman, got the explanation.

The battalion chief shook his head, his mouth a thin, grim line. "The guy that saved you must have been somebody else."

The boy was frantic. "Jeez! I'm telling you…."

A feeble groan from Wentworth, prostrate on the ground, whirled all three toward him. He had tossed an arm upward. He rolled his head, opened his eyes, closed them again. The boy dropped to his knees.

"Wake up, Mister," he pleaded, shaking Wentworth's shoulder. "Wake up. These guys say you threw them bombs. Wake up and tell them you didn't."

THE BOY'S words stabbed into Wentworth's brain. His mind groped back toward full consciousness. But he gave no indication that he had heard. He rolled his head again, mumbled sounds. He thought frantically, battling the terrific pain that ripped his head like hot knives. He had gone into the warehouse, seen a bomber… that was it. He had been slugged. For once the Spider, shorn of his friends by the necessity of remaining in hiding, separated from his chief sources of strength, worn by his strenuous rescues and escapes, had fallen prey to a lesser man. But the bombs? Obviously a plant, a frame-up.

He opened his eyes fully, stared up at the lurid sky, saw the boy's pale anxious face. Wentworth forced his body up with his arms.

"Wha-what happened?" he mumbled.

The boy poured out his story in an eager rush. "Now these dumb clucks," he jerked a grimy, disdainful thumb over his shoulder at the firemen, "are trying to say you set the place on fire, just because they found a glass thingamabob on you."

"There's some mistake," he told the two men slowly. "I know nothing of the bombs. What the boy says is true. I did rescue him and his family. Then I saw fire just starting in that warehouse. I went in to see what I could do, ran into a man and fought with him. He slugged me. If you found a bomb on me, it was planted there."

The battalion chief was a stubby man with a stubby face. He wrinkled a round red nose in disbelief. "Hooey," he said, "plain hooey!"

Wentworth dropped his hands. He still swayed on his feet, but it was deliberate. He did not want his captors to know how swiftly he was regaining his strength.

"Surely, you don't think I'm one of those fiends!" he exclaimed. "Why would I save this boy and his family if I were throwing the bombs? It doesn't make sense."

The man's stubby face set stubbornly. "There's nobody but you and the boy says you saved them," he grunted. "You come along."

Wentworth stared at him with eyes that masked his swiftly racing thoughts. He swung his head slowly from side to side as if dazed. Actually he was scanning the possibilities of escape. Firemen were on all sides. Four policemen were striding forward with leveled guns. Run? Not a chance… now. He was weak—and there was nowhere to run except back into the fire.

"But you can't do this!" he cried.

The fire chief grunted. The boy thrust in between Wentworth and his accusers. "Sure, you can't do it!" he declared. "I tell you this guy…."

Wentworth's hand rested lightly on his shoulder. "It does no good, old man," he said gently. "Thanks just the same."

He turned the boy about and shook his hand gravely, bent toward him in a completely serious bow. His lips did not move, but Wentworth poured words out rapidly. The boy's face was startled for a second, then, his back to the officers, he winked deliberately. He jerked his head in a quick nod.

"Just the same," the boy declared, "they can't get away with this. I'm going to tell mom to tell our alderman."

He whipped his hand free of Wentworth's and darted away among the welter of sprawling hose.

THE POLICE surrounded Wentworth cautiously, pistols drawn. Two of them clapped hands on his shoulders.

"So this is the firebug?" one growled. He slashed Wentworth across the back of the skull with his pistol barrel. It crashed like red hot iron on the old wound. Wentworth bit down a cry, reeled forward and would have plunged to his knees except for the hands upon his shoulders.

"You can't take it, huh?" The cop's voice was grating in his ear. We'll have a chance to find out when we get to headquarters. You might—fall down the stairs."

Wentworth let his head sag forward. He knew all about that fall down stairs. It was the familiar excuse when police cut loose on a man with lengths of rubber hose and paper-wrapped nightsticks. Wentworth knew he would be in for it, because of the villainous crime of which he was accused. If he were herded into headquarters, it was unlikely his demand that Kirkpatrick be called would be heeded… not until Wentworth had been thoroughly beaten.

And Kirkpatrick could do little good. Already Wentworth stood accused of murder. If he revealed his identity, this new arrest, with a fire bomb on his person, would be only another damning link in the chain against him.

Never had Wentworth fought against such overwhelming odds, he had been arrested and accused before but never had the evidence seemed so damaging. Never had he been so completely severed from his resources, cut off from Nita, from Ram Singh, from Professor Brownlee and his mechanical wizardry. Never had he been so without clues as in this battle against criminals who sought to ravage the country of food, even to the point of the starvation of the populace for their own selfish ends.

Despite the police and the Spider, the major objective of the Food Destroyers had been accomplished. Huge stores of edibles had been ruined with flame and water. Tomorrow's market would reflect the destruction in soaring prices. And the people would suffer.

Out toward the police lines Wentworth was taken. A crowd of thousands was pressed against a hastily stretched rope, staring into the area of devastation. Toward them, Wentworth was carried from the dim pall of smoke, a stumbling, half dazed figure ringed by police.

A murmur ran through the crowd. Those in back strained to peer at the prisoner. The murmur grew louder. Then a shrill voice piped: "Lynch him! Lynch him! It's the firebug!"

OVER TO the left of the crowd, another shrill voice picked up the cry. A rock whizzed through the air and bounded toward Wentworth. He stopped in his tracks, raising a fright-distorted face. He strained back against his captors.

"Lynch the firebug!" the shrill voice persisted.

The murmur of the crowd mounted, became a threatening rumble as of an approaching storm. The police stood tensely, surveying the crowd with wary eyes. Other police were strung along the front of the crowd, reinforcing the rope, but if that mob cut loose, the scanty guard would not be able to damn it. They would be tossed aside like chips on the breast of a dam-smashing flood.

"Don't let them get me," Wentworth whimpered. He flapped his arms helplessly, still swaying as if half-dazed on his feet. "Don't let them get me!"

The thunderous rumble of the crowd deepened. The shrill piping insistence of a voice cried through it. "Lynch the firebug!" The shrill demand found supporters. Deeper voices caught it up. "Lynch him! Lynch him!"

"Take me away," Wentworth pleaded with the police. "Don't let them lynch me!"

"Shut up," a cop muttered.

Wentworth could barely hear the words above the roar of the mob. The close packed ranks were like a gale-torn sea now, white, tossing faces, fists and arms hurled aloft like flotsam on the waves. Individual words were lost in the vast incoherent roar of its anger. Slowly the police who held Wentworth began to inch away from the terror of the pack. They walked backward with guns drawn. Their holds on Wentworth relaxed. He crowded close to them, pleading.

The haze of the smoke reached out, threw veils before them. The shouts of the mob crescendoed. Their prey was escaping. A furious volley of pistol shots! Through the thickening night, Wentworth saw the crowd pour over the rope. Men caught it up and raced on with it stretched out before them as if it were a talisman that would overpower all obstacles.

"Lynch! Lynch! Lynch!" the voice of the mob chanted.

The police turned and ran for it, scrambled towards a smoldering brick wall. Wentworth ran with them. They did not even grip his arms. So deeply had he wrought his fears upon their minds that they never thought of his leaving them. He moved as a part of their body. He crouched when they crouched. He ran when they ran. He took cover with them behind a fire crumbled brick wall.

On, the mob surged. The hiding place of the fugitives was

discovered. Shots belched from police guns, over the heads of the crowd. The mob rushed on. Their own guns spoke answer. Brick chips flew from the barricade. A policeman reeled away from the wall, cursing, his hand gripping his shoulder.

Wentworth cowered among the tumbled, hot bricks. The cops continued to fire into the air. He saw them put their heads together. They were debating turning over to the pack. He smiled thinly. It was the moment he had awaited. He sprang to the barricade where the mob could see him plainly. The police whirled to stare at him, threw up their guns and hesitated.

Wentworth, standing fully exposed to the guns of the on-rushing mob, waved one hand above his head—waved gaily, as if in friendly greeting!

CHAPTER 11
—INTO THE FIRE

WENTWORTH'S GESTURE was a ridiculous, gamin antic. It startled the police who stood with ready guns. It startled the mob that howled for his blood. But it was a calculated thing. For an instant, it stopped the attack dead.

In that instant, Wentworth, his strength recuperated now, sprang to the street and sprinted to the nearest corner. He had spun around it and was racing off into the blackness before the amazed mob could gather itself together and fling forward.

The sea of the mob poured across the street, reached the corner where Wentworth had disappeared and streamed around it with a sullen roar. Block after block it flowed until it beat out its fury in breathless exertion, until panting and baffled, the crowd began to disintegrate. First twos and threes dropped out, then scores until finally only a handful raced on through dark hopeless streets. Finally their gallop slowed to a walk. They stared at each other, stared around into motionless, unrelenting blackness, cursed and went away wearily.

The Spider had vanished into the night from which he had come.

While the mob pounded the streets, he threaded his way through cellars and rubbish-jammed backyards, through broken boards in fences, following on the heels of a boy of twelve whose eyes were bright with excitement and whose voice was hoarse from shouter.

"Did I do all right?" he demanded when finally the roar of the mob had subsided into a distant murmur.

"You did fine," Wentworth told him. "By siccing that mob onto me with your shout of, 'Lynch the firebug,' you broke the police lines so that I could slip out and gave me the interruption I needed. When I get out of this mess, you're going to hear from me."

"Aw, gee," said the boy. "Don't talk like that. Me and you is pals. You save me. I save you!"

"Noblesse oblige," Wentworth murmured.

"What?"

"I was just saying," Wentworth told him quietly, "that no man has a higher code of honor than that. Shake, pal."

The boy thrust out his hand. "Me name's Timothy Walsh," he said gravely "What's yours?"

Wentworth slipped from his finger a ring. It was a plain gold signet with a single gold initial on it. He took his cigarette lighter from his pocket and pressed its base to the gold seal of the ring. When he had taken the cigarette lighter away, a spot glowed red upon the gold.

He handed the ring to the boy, holding his eyes. "That's a dangerous momenta," he said. "Let no one see it, but if you ever need help, send that to Stanley Kirkpatrick, commissioner of police, and I'll come."

He clasped hands with the boy again and faded into the shadows. Tim stood looking after him awhile, then stared down at the ring he clasped tightly in his hand. He couldn't see it clearly and held it up to a vagrant beam of a street light that strayed into the yard where he stood. His mouth dropped open with a gasp. His eyes fairly bulged. He stared off into the darkness where Wentworth had gone, then back to the ring.

Timothy gulped, tried to speak, gulped again.

"Geez!" he got out tremulously, "Geez! *He was the Spider!*"

The spot of red that glowed on the ring, the spot that Wentworth had printed on his platinum signet, was the hairy legged *seal of the Spider!*

Timothy Walsh clasped the ring in the palm of his hand, whirled and ran at top speed into the night....

Wentworth was smiling quietly to himself as he stole off, beyond the police lines now and circling through the cluttered streets of the east side.

IN THE morning, a black cloak draped over a hunched shoulder, his violin under his arm, and a drooping black hat drawn over lank, black hair, Wentworth rode the subway to a corner near the home of Janice Hally in an apartment house in the west Eighties.

Two blocks from the girl's home, he halted on the curb, faced the buildings and set his violin case at his feet. He lifted the instrument out, brushed block cords from the strings and, tuning it, began sweet music. He stood there playing in the sunshine of a spring morning. March had forgotten its cold blasts overnight and now spilled gold upon this queer hunch-shouldered figure draped in black, his beaked nose intent over the sounding violin.

Children scampering along the streets stopped and gaped at him. Windows opened, and heads appeared. But it was not until coins began to jingle down on the sidewalk about him that Wentworth realized his audience.

He collected the coins gravely—some worthy charity should receive them—and moved up the block. So he marched and played, and marched again, while urchins and children with nursemaids moved with him. Always he kept his eyes swinging toward the apartment house up the street where Janice Hally, his red-headed Nemesis lived. Sometime today Nita Van Sloan, his Nita, would be going there bent on getting the Hally girl's promise to withdraw her charges, so that the Spider once more could battle in the open.

Wentworth passed a small, red-fronted store with placarded prices in the windows. Already they were zooming. Sugar 120, Coffee 750. Little things, but this was only the beginning. The fire demons had struck only twice here and the pinch had not yet reached the huge piled supplies of chain groceries. But already prices on two staples had doubled. High prices, then poverty, then famine, lean-jawed and swollen-bellied, bony stilts for legs, stalking through the land.

Wentworth's mouth went grim beneath the hawk-like beak he had made of his nose. His eyes held ugly lights. And the music that he wrenched now from his violin was violent and stormy. As ever, his mood communicated itself to his instrument. Harsh resounding chords soared. There was anger in their sound.

Windows slammed down. Nurses jerked their children away with backward glares at this gnome of a man who did such things with a violin. A cop who had ignored him previously stalked toward him with swinging club, a deliberateness about his pace that boded ill for the old music maker.

Wentworth spotted him coming, changed his music to saccharine inoffensiveness. When the cop still was a hundred feet away, he swung into an Irish jig. The cop paused opposite him, stared uncertain a moment, then moved on along his beat, his stick tapping unconscious time to the jig against his leg.

A taxi droned into the street and Wentworth, catching up his case, moved directly in front of the apartment of Janice Hally, started once more to play. The taxi halted beside him and Nita got out, Nita trim in a blue-tailored suit and rich black furs, a jaunty black straw saucy upon her chestnut curls. She paid off the taxi, stopped a moment to listen to the music. WENTWORTH PLAYED on, wooden-faced, never glancing at her until he had finished, then he walked toward her with hat outstretched for alms. Nita put her hand into her purse and hesitated, inspecting him keenly with her brilliant eyes.

"Your music is very familiar, Maestro," she said. "You play very much like someone I know."

Wentworth drew back his hat. *"Pardon, Signora,* but that ees not possible. Someone else play like thee great Tito Caliepi? *Bah!"*

When the Policeman strolled past, watchful again, she was saying: "Indeed, you play too well to have to go about the streets like this. If you will give me your name and address, I'll see if I can't do something about it—some recitals at teas or something."

Wentworth stopped his playing. *"Gracias, Signora.* You are as generous as you are beautiful." He dropped into Italian, spilling out words like exclamations while he scribbled his name and address upon a card and handed it to her. To the cop it was more protestations of thankfulness at the woman's help. But Wentworth was telling Nita swiftly to set Ram Singh to trailing Janice Hally for a possible clue to the Food Destroyers.

He smiled with a final bow. "Just the sight of you, *Signorina,"* he concluded, "is an inspiration that will never fail. I feel as strong as a thousand men, now. My violin…." He snatched it up and began to play a love song.

Nita smiled and strode into the house. Wentworth played his way on up the street.

Fifteen minutes passed. A half hour. The tiny pucker of a frown disturbed Wentworth's forehead. His worried eyes strayed time and again to the apartment where Nita had entered. Forty-five minutes passed.

There shivered through Wentworth the premonition of evil. He felt the awakening of a reddening pulse in the thin white scar upon his temple. Abruptly he terminated his music, put the violin in its case and circled the block to the rear of the apartment house. A vacant lot, where a house had been torn down, admitted him to the rear court. He began once more to play. He got an audience, but no sign of Nita.

The shivering apprehension became a cold tingle along Wentworth's spine, a certainty of disaster. Nita would have recognized the music, known that he wanted word with her and at least waved from a window. He knew that. The only answer was that she was not able to reach a window, and that….

Wentworth moved toward the next building. His audience evaporated, and he ducked into a cellar entrance, made his way upward into the apartment house into which Nita had vanished. He found Janice Hally's apartment number, climbed steep stairs to a door numbered 6H.

HE HEARD voices within, a man's whining and shrill, a woman's protesting. Once in a while another woman spoke. But he could hear no words. Wentworth peered about. A fire exit opened to the rear. He made his way rapidly to it. No one in sight. He got out, moved along the fire escape to a window that opened into Janice Hally's apartment. The shade was drawn. He listened intently.

The man's voice rose shrilly: "I tell you it is the only way. Get out of here, and I'll toss a bomb under her chair." The voice changed to high laughter, a little mad. Such laughter as Wentworth had heard before, the laughter of the dope fiend he had surprised about to attack Xavier Jones!

Wentworth's eyes became hard as agate, his lips compressed into colorless lines.

The addict's voice shrilled on. "The flames won't make her easy to identify. They'll think she's you!"

"No, no!" a girl's voice cut in.

"Yes!" said the shrilled-voiced man.

"He's crazy, Miss Hally, crazy! In heaven's name…."

That was Nita.

Wentworth waited no longer. He thrust the violin case through the window pane and dived in behind it, pistol in hand. The room was dark. His sun-dazzled eyes made out three figures vaguely, a girl that must be Nita in a chair, two other figures moving.

"Stand still!" he grated harshly.

A man's voice ripped out in a shrill cry of terror. "The Spider! The Spider!" He darted toward the door.

Wentworth threw up his gun, but held his fire. The man was more valuable alive, if he could be traced when Ram Singh took up Janice Hally's trail.

Wentworth's eyes were completely accustomed to the gloom now. He saw that Nita's arms were bound to a heavy chair in which she was seated. Beyond her, half-crouched, fear and hate white upon her face, stood Janice Hally, her red hair like fire in the darkness of the room.

"The Spider!" she whispered. And the two words were like a curse.

Wentworth moved slowly to Nita, freed her swiftly with his pocketknife. His eyes never left the other girl and when he had severed the last rope, he crossed toward her with the gun leveled in his hand.

"You are going with me," he said softly. "There are things you know which will help me in my work."

"Murderer!" the girl threw at him. Her lips were tight against her teeth.

Wentworth nodded genially. "Now if this other young lady will tie you up?"

Nita came from behind him, ropes in her hands. She moved purposefully toward the other girl, but she did not get between the gun and its target.

"Hurry!" Wentworth bit out. "That damned idiot that ran away...."

Abruptly Janice threw back her head with its weight of red hair and laughed. "You're too late. Too late!" she chanted.

She pointed toward the door. Wentworth did not take his eyes from her, his gun did not swerve aside. "What's she pointing at, Miss?"

Nita's head swung toward the door. Her eyes widened, words jerked from her; "There's smoke seeping under the door, black smoke. It looks as if.... That crazy loon threw a fire bomb."

Wentworth cursed, strode toward the door. Behind him there was a brief, stamping tussle and Janice plunged toward the back

Nita Van Sloan

window of the apartment through which Wentworth had dived. He raced after her, three yards behind.

"Halt!" he ordered. "Halt, or I'll shoot!"

Janice ran on. Her foot caught on the violin case and, with a half-smothered cry, she pitched forward. Her head glanced against a chair arm and she crumpled limply to the floor. Wentworth caught himself, dropped beside her on the floor, his hand going swiftly to her temple. The pulse was there, strong, but a little fluttery.

He caught the girl up. "Bring my violin, Nita, please," he asked and hastened toward the door. He caught the knob with the hand that was beneath Janice's knees tugged it open—reeled back gasping. The hall was a mass of curling, leaping flames! A tongue of it shot into the room, seared Wentworth's hands. He kicked the door shut, staggered against it, gasping for breath.

He straightened, raced toward the window, Nita behind him. At his quick head gesture, Nita flung up the shade. They peered out together, and Nita's hand closed in tight panic on Wentworth's arm.

"Oh, Dick, Dick!" she moaned. "You're trapped. Look!"

Pounding along the vacant foundations behind the apartment

house, racing toward, the building from which Wentworth sought to escape with his prisoner, were two policemen. One of them was the cop who already had shown suspicion of the old violin player!

CHAPTER 12
THE SPIDER FALLS

WENTWORTH, STARING at the racing policemen, knew that even as Nita spoke, they were trapped.

"It's all right," he said calmly. "Those cops will be easy. Climb out."

Nita hesitated. "But one is the policeman that stared at you so suspiciously out in front. He'll recognize you," she insisted. "He'll want to know how you happened to be in here."

"Climb out," Wentworth repeated.

Nita reluctantly sat upon the sill, drew up her knees and whirled her feet to the fire escape. Carrying the violin, she stepped aside while Wentworth toiled after her with the unconscious girl. He held his left shoulder hunched and struggled with his load as if he were feeble.

"Here's an explanation for the cops, Nita," he said swiftly. "You called me in to arrange music for a tea you're planning next week. Now hurry. Be careful with that violin. Don't press that end fastening."

Nita nodded, descended the open grill stairs gingerly, glancing up as Wentworth followed with the girl. They reached the lowest landing, released the ladder to the ground and climbed down. The police were upon them instantly.

"What's the matter here?"

Wentworth turned toward the two, the girl face down over his shoulder now. He threw out a swiftly gesturing arm. "Smoke!" he exclaimed. "She must go to a hospital, quick!"

A cop stalked beside him. "What were you doing up in that apartment, anyway? I thought…."

Nita was hurrying along beside them. She broke in on the questioning. "I called him up about music for a tea I'm planning. He's really a very good violinist."

The cop turned his frown on Nita, scowling red, heavy brows. "Yeah—And I gotta take your word for that I guess?"

Nita's haughty stare disconcerted the cop. He turned his eyes away, mumbled. "I can't take no chances, ma'am."

"You can keep a civil tongue in your head," Nita snapped.

Wentworth struggled out to the sidewalk. Up near the corner, an engine buzzed into life, a yellow taxi spurted toward them. Wentworth heaved the girl into the tonneau, gestured excitedly to Nita.

"Quick! Hurry! The Hospital!"

Nita got in carrying Wentworth's violin case and he put his foot upon the running board. A policeman's hand bit into his shoulder.

"Not so fast, buddy. We got some questions to ask you."

Wentworth whirled, spitting out Italian explosively. He waved his hands in the air. "It won't work," he told Nita, in Italian.

"Take the girl to your home, get Ram Singh to bring her and you to my room tonight. You have the address. Hurry."

THE TAXI lurched forward. The cop opened a wide mouth to yell, hesitated. The girl was unconscious and he feared consequences. He let the cab whine around a corner and buzz northward, then spun savagely on Wentworth.

"You won't get away!" he declared vehemently. "Not until I find out what you were doing in that building."

Wentworth hugged the violin case to him, and his thin-jawed, hook-nosed face smiled. He shrugged a shoulder. The police marched him around the block to the front of the building. Three red fire trucks were packed into the street and pressure stuffed hoses led into the building. A crowd was held back by police.

Above the clanking and the purr of engines, a shrill voice rang out:

"They've caught the Spider! The Spider!" it keened. "They've caught the Spider!"

Police whirled to stare into the close packed ranks of the crowd, seeking to single out the unseen accuser. They found no one, but Wentworth knew who had called, and his jaw muscles made his thin cheek even leaner. That was the pasty-faced dope addict who had set the apartment house afire, who had wanted to kill Nita.

Wentworth stood impassively as if the words meant nothing to him. The police stared at him and held their guns rigidly. He could read their thoughts. If this was the Spider, there was a huge reward just around the corner for them. It behooved them to be careful. They called reinforcements.

"The Spider! The Spider!" the police jabbered.

Six guns covered Wentworth. A patrol wagon clanged to the corner and the police formed a ring and marched him toward it. He still fondled his violin case.

As Wentworth and his escort neared the patrol, a seventh cop swung from the front seat, stalked back and unlocked the door. They all stood aside with ready guns to watch Wentworth enter. He hunched more drearily over his violin case. His hand fumbled at the upper catch and, without warning, from its smaller end a jet of grayish vapor spewed out. Wentworth made a swift turn and the tear gas spat into the face of every one of the seven cops. They yelled with surprise, with the smarting pain of the gas.

Wentworth dropped the violin case which burst, releasing thickening clouds of the gas. He darted behind the patrol, ran along its left side. They had searched him vainly for a pistol, but Wentworth caught one now from the crown of his wide-brimmed black hat and thrust it against the neck of the driver.

"Go like hell!" he ordered.

The driver took one white-faced look and jammed the accelerator to the running board. The bulky patrol wagon jerked forward. Wentworth sprang off, ran for cover. They would expect him to escape on the patrol. If he were quick to reach that alley…. Guns banged behind. A numbing blow on Wentworth's left shoulder sent him reeling headlong, almost threw him to the earth.

He uttered no sound, but his lips curled back from his teeth and his face went white. A police bullet had drilled his left shoulder. He ran on, found a door and fumblingly picked the lock, made his slow, painful way through the dim basement of another apartment. Moments later he ducked into a subway station, rode uptown on the dark clanging platform of a train. Warm blood trickled from his wound. He was thankful for the black cloak that hid it. A dizzy lightness invaded his brain. He fought it back, left the train after two stops and took a cross-town bus to the east side.

HE MOVED in a daze now, but the flow of blood had stopped. His shirt had plugged the wound. The numbness of the blow gave way to a burning ache. His shoulder seemed enormous. His ears buzzed with weakness from loss of blood. He staggered off the bus, got a taxi and sped to his room, climbed stairs laboriously and fumbled the door open.

His lips were grimly locked. He tugged off his hat and cape, ran hot water into a bowl and stripped the clothing from the upper half of his body, staring at the wound.

The bullet had smashed all the way through. It had drained well, but he knew from its position that cartilage had been broken. It would be days before he could use that arm, weeks before it regained its strength. He gulped whisky from a flask, proceeded systematically with bathing the wound with hot water in which iodine had been dropped, fitted an awkward bandage. It would do until Nita and Ram Singh could come.

Not until then did he sink upon his bed. He fought off the

sleep of fatigue, battled against the buzzing dizziness in his head.

Finally, he thrust himself up from the bed with his one good arm. He sat for a moment weakly, pain throbbing through his wound. Two and a half hours since he had dispatched Nita with Janice Hally a prisoner. It could not have taken this long to get her home, summon Ram Singh and come to Wentworth's room. Something somewhere had miscarried.

He straightened with an effort; raised a clenched fist to his forehead, pressing against the ache of it. Wounded, fever, and Nita in peril, the Food Destroyers ravaging the city. Unless they were exterminated, famine would follow.

Wentworth knew famine. A strong shudder shook him. He had seen it in France in the war. Ten year old children the size of three years with ancient, wizened faces, skin that clung to the bones of arms and legs, hunger-bloated bellies. A woman and a man snarling like dogs in a tooth and nail battle for a crust of moldy bread. He remembered a child he had fed, furtive as a wild animal, trembling with eagerness. Its hunger-maddened eyes rose up before him....

He stopped in the middle of the floor, swaying. The window! There was someone outside the window! White teeth. With an inarticulate cry, Wentworth wheeled staggering, plunged toward his revolver. He stumbled, stretched his length on the floor, crawled forward on his belly toward the gun.

He heard the window flung open. Footsteps clumped on the floor. Wentworth rolled over on his back with a choked, scream, threw up his hands. A man's shadow fell across him.

The man dropped on his knees beside Wentworth. He wore a turban and his dark face was troubled.

Ram Singh caught Wentworth by the shoulder, shook him slightly. "Master," he urged. "Listen closely, in the name of the holiest. The *Missie Sahib* is in the hands of the police. She is behind bars. The police found your address in her purse. They are on the way!"

Wentworth tossed, moaning. "Take it away," he pleaded.

Ram Singh caught him by both shoulders and Wentworth gasped out in pain. The Hindu's swift fingers found the wound then. He flashed a single swift look about the room, snatched Wentworth's black cloak and flung it about him, then caught up his delirious master in his powerful arms and stepped out the window.

Heavy footsteps pounded through the hall behind. A fist pounded peremptorily at the door.

"Open up," a gruff voice ordered.

Ram Singh ran catfooted across a shed roof beneath the window, clambered down to the ground and ducked into an alley. A head with a uniformed cap thrust out the window. A gun glinted. But Ram Singh had vanished into the black shadows with Wentworth, only half-conscious, in his arms.

CHAPTER 13
FAMINE STALKS THE CITY

S UPPORTING WENTWORTH as if he were drunk, Ram Singh took a taxi and rode to an auto rental garage where he obtained a car. He transferred Wentworth to it and raced northward along the Albany road. Nowhere in the city was there succor for the hunted Spider and Ram Singh took his master to the only friend he had who could be trusted now that Nita was in prison. He took Wentworth to Professor Brownlee near Croton-on Hudson.

Wentworth was in a raging fever when he reached the small white cottage of Professor Brownlee. He did not recognize the cheery-faced savant with his twinkling eyes and graying van dyke beard, as Ram Singh helped his reeling master from the car. His head sagged, his eyes were glassy and his parched lips mumbled meaningless sounds. Brownlee's smile vanished in consternation. With Ram Singh's help, the little professor got Wentworth in bed and examined the wound. It was redly inflamed. He went to work.

There were flashes when Wentworth opened his eyes sanely and knew the attentive Ram Singh and Professor, but they were brief and it was three weeks before the fever left him, and he recognized the neat low-ceiling bed room in which he lay. There were worn shadows beneath his eyes as he turned them on Professor Brownlee's beaming face. Wentworth smiled faintly. "The wound... proved feverish... eh?" he asked.

Brownlee nodded briskly.

"How long?" Wentworth demanded.

The professor shook his head, still smiling, held out medicine.

His patient twisted his head aside. "How long?" he insisted. He turned back and his eyes grew feverish, his thin white hands plucked at the blankets.

The professor's bearded lips pursed. He said slowly: "Three weeks."

Wentworth tossed on the bed, thrust himself up. "I… must… go!" His arms collapsed under him and he fell back weakly. "I… can't…" It was a cry.

The professor offered the medicine again. "Sleep is the thing, Dick. In another week, you'll be out of this."

"A week!"

Brownlee leaned forward, frowning, his brown eyes serious. "Listen, Dick," he said. "I know how important it is for you to be able to battle. But if you go back to the attack weak, without your full strength, you will fail. You cannot win against this gang you are fighting with anything less than your full faculties. You know that. Now, be sensible."

Wentworth bit his lips. He forced the fever from his mind. "You are right, of course," he conceded slowly. "I must… get my strength. Hurry, Professor… the life of the nation itself…."

Brownlee nodded, proffered the medicine again and Wentworth sank into sleep.

Three weeks ill. Another week before the Spider could battle again…. The professor shook his head slowly at Ram Singh. He looked haggard-eyed.

"I doubt," he whispered, "I doubt that even Dick can help now."

THREE WEEKS…. The red serpent of flame had writhed through the packed streets of New York. Charred ruins scarred its waterfronts. Grain elevators had rolled dense smoke into the sky; ship loads of sugars and coffees had burned at the docks; warehouses of canned goods had been destroyed. Lighters ferrying produce across the Hudson from Jersey had ignited in midstream. Fully two thousand lives had been sacrificed in the mad march of Food Destroyers.

These things Wentworth learned when he began to recuperate, learned how Ram Singh had saved him. Beside these facts, the news of his own indictment for murder became a trivial thing. But Nita, Nita in jail for complicity in the apartment house fire. That enraged him! "Glastonbury shall pay for that," he swore.

The whole world cried out for vengeance. The fires of hell had not been confined to New York. All over the country, the torch had been applied. Wheat fields in the west had been swept by consuming flashes; grain elevators along the Great Lakes; Chicago stock yards had been laid waste, thousands of cattle destroyed; warehouses in New Orleans, docks in San Francisco. In Cuba, sugar plantations had burned... the tale of the damage was endless. And in the cities prices soared and soared. They became unbelievable. It seemed the Destroyers had done their work almost too well, but that was not so.

Food still trickled into the cities, food that commanded fabulous figures. The government rationed and distributed supplies. It was another war time, but a war that tore the nation within itself. Soldiers guarded supplies, but whenever accumulating goods threatened to become sufficient to needs, the bombers struck again, and there was want. The head of every company in the world connected in any way with producing or distributing food was examined and questioned to no avail. No clue to the monster behind the outrages was found.

These things Wentworth learned slowly from the newspapers and Professor Brownlee during that week of recuperation which alone he allowed himself. The professor turned all his marvelous scientific ability to the task of building him up and at the end of the week, still gaunt and thin, but gaining in strength and health daily, Wentworth and Ram Singh, disguised as truck drivers, reentered the city of New York.

Wentworth had been prepared for disaster, he had been prepared for mob violence, for famine, but his imagination could not picture the catastrophe that had shaken the nation. New York was a city without gayety, almost without life. People moved furtively through the streets. Children were too listless or too weak to play. They moped about with thinning cheeks, legs gone bony with hunger. Wentworth had loaded the tarpaulin-covered truck he rode with wood, but as they trundled down upper Broadway, Ram Singh careless-seeming behind the wheel, a shouting mob of men charged from a side street, swarmed on the running board waving threatening clubs.

Wentworth stood: "I've got nothing but a load of wood," he shouted.

He stared at the men. They were wild-eyed, haggard-faced. Many were unshaven and their clothing filthy. Food had gone and with it their morale. Why shave, why wash when a growling belly twisted in pain for lack of food, when your wife and children were too weak to do anything but sit and stare pitifully, their sunken eyes asking what their lips no longer dared articulate: "Food!"

Three men sprang to the rear of the truck, ripped up the tarpaulin, exposed the wood. The crowd in front mouthed threats. You're a farmer, ain't you? Why don't you raise food!"

"Let's string up the damned farmer!"

Ram Singh sent the truck lurching forward. Men scrambled from their path. Bricks and clubs pelted the vehicle. Wentworth's gaunt jaws clenched. He saw a store smashed in and robbed, the soldier guard clubbed to the earth. Somewhere in this city, he knew, were the fiends responsible for this horror. They were self-confident now, rulers of the world, believing that even the Spider who had harassed them for a while, was dead.

The trail? The trail led first to Janice Hally. Only she of the dozens who labored for the Food Destroyers was known to him. From her must stem the clue that would lead to the gang's ultimate downfall: True, there was Xavier Jones and the threat against him, but there the trail was indirect and speed was essential. No, Janice Hally was the only clue.

WENTWORTH AND Ram Singh abandoned the truck, went to the apartment building were Janice Hally had lived. She was no longer there. The superintendent said she had not returned since the fire. Since the fire, since Nita's arrest... Wentworth's sunken eyes gleamed. He stood facing Ram Singh in the furnished room they had taken in Harlem. He was still a figure of a man to arrest attention, tall, broad-shouldered, with the alive, alert face of a man who knows life and loves it.

There was command in the piercing gray eyes. There was a fire there, too, a fire that seemed a little mad....

"Ram Singh," he said slowly. "Rent a car and have it here in an hour." He outlined swiftly his clothing needs. "At eight o'clock I am going to call on District Attorney Glastonbury!"

Ram Singh's head came up sharply, protest in his face. Wentworth's grim thin-mouthed face brooked no opposition. His illness, stripping off all surplus flesh had exposed its full craggy power. His nose was thinly dominant, his chin jutting. Such a face must have been a Caesar's when he faced the rebellious Legions. Ram Singh bowed submission, sweeping palms to his forehead.

"When the *sahib* says do this, it is performed!"

He whirled and left. Wentworth waited five minutes, then left also. He rode a subway to Times Square, entered a booth with a dial phone and called a lawyer friend, put him to work on freeing Nita.

"Spare no expense," Wentworth ordered. "Use every means in your power."

He hung up then and immediately phoned Glastonbury.

"Richard Wentworth speaking." He said and smiled thinly at the gasp, the beginnings of a tirade. "Just a minute," he cut in shortly, "Save that. What time are you going to be at your office tonight?" Once more the twisted lips mocked a smile. "From now on, eh? Anxious, Glastonbury?... Yes, I had a reason for asking. I'm going to pay you a visit. Surrender?" Wentworth laughed sharply. "Surrender is an ugly work. I prefer, as I said, to pay you a visit."

He hung up, left the booth quickly and took the subway back to his room. When Ram Singh came, he attired himself faultlessly in Tuxedo, pulled a black fedora over his brows and went directly to the closed car the Hindu had rented. He settled himself back comfortably into the cushions, wincing as his healing shoulder gave him a twinge.

Ram Singh sent the car rolling downtown. Wentworth closed his eyes in thought. Beneath his left arm nestled once more the tool kit of the Spider. In his coat pocket reposed a compact automatic. Yes, all things were in order.

WENTWORTH SEEMED asleep, yet when the car braked to a careful halt two blocks from the apartment home of Glastonbury, his eyes opened instantly. He climbed to the walk deliberately, nodded to Ram Singh.

"The usual arrangements, Ram Singh," he said briefly. "I expect to remain until my good friend Glastonbury wearies of waiting in his office and comes home." He smiled thinly. "It's a surprise."

Ram Singh touched his forehead, *"Han, Sahib!"* and as Wentworth walked calmly down the street stared with burning eyes after his master. Always the *sahib* did things that seemed a little mad, always things of utmost daring. But he was not yet of sound health and this seemed maddest of all. A man indicted for murder, hunted throughout the nation, walking calmly into the District Attorney's home!

Walking? Wentworth was sauntering, swinging a cane and he stepped into the entrance of the apartment where Glastonbury made his home. He glanced carelessly at the name directory in the hall, strolled to the elevator. Glastonbury's quarters were on the twelfth floor.

"Fifteen," said Wentworth, and, when the elevator had descended, walked down three flights, used a lockpick as readily as an ordinary man would a key and walked in. A startled Filipino boy with sleek black hair stared at him with white-rimmed eyes. Wentworth nodded casually.

"Mr. Glastonbury will he back later. I'm to make myself at home until he returns," he smiled. "Where is this Scotch he brags about?"

The Filipino smiled uncertainly, ducked a bow and started off.

"No ice, please," Wentworth called after him, seated himself in an easy chair, placing stick and hat beside him, and picked up a book. He did not even glance up when the boy returned with decanter and siphon.

It was an hour before Wentworth laid the book down, glanced up to discover the Filipino still standing patiently in the doorway. Wentworth yawned, patting his mouth. "Where's the library?" he asked. The boy led the way, switched on lights and Wentworth prowled along the shelves. The boy left.

In two minutes, Wentworth had located a cylindrical safe masked by books. It took him five more—stethoscopic suction disc attached to its face recorded the faint clicks of the lock—to open it. He replaced books in front of the safe and strolled into sight of the boy again, inspecting books, took down an old court journal, and moved across the door again.

With silk gloved hands to prevent finger prints, he stripped the safe, found a notebook which showed that Janice Hally was under guard at the Marlborough Hotel as a witness, the names of her guards, her phone number.

Wentworth smiled at the thoroughness of the little game-cock district attorney. He returned the notebook to its shelf. This was what he had come for. There were other legal documents with a rubber band about them labeled with the girl's name. Wentworth glanced at these curiously. They were affidavits accusing him of the Yonkers fire, accusing Nita of the apartment fire, both signed by Janice Hally.

Wentworth smiled grimly, his eyes hard. Easy to destroy these damaging documents, but he shook his head. His eyes glinting, he placed the papers between the sheets of the ancient law journal, relocked the safe and placed the leather-bound book on its high rack.

HE SELECTED another book at random, strolled out again to his seat beside the decanter, and waited for Glastonbury as calmly as for a drink. Scarcely the demeanor of a man indicted for murder, a man who had just burglarized the safe of the district attorney, waiting for the owner to return. He leaned back his head and closed his eyes.

Two hours later, District Attorney Glastonbury came home, pounded his hard leather heels across the floor and brought up with an open mouth, staring at Wentworth, comfortable beside his decanter. Wentworth opened his eyes, rose and bowed to Glastonbury.

"You! You!" Words stuck in the throat of the district attorney. His diminutive energy-packed body fairly contorted with anger. He rose on his toes, his face reddening.

Wentworth looked at him curiously, "Have you ever been warned of apoplexy?" he asked.

Glastonbury exploded with a splutter of words. "Of all the unadulterated nerve, of all the preposterous—"

Wentworth stood casually. The Filipino boy was staring with jerking eyes from one to the other of the men. Wentworth turned to him. "Another glass," he said. The boy's mouth sagged open, but he darted off. Wentworth took his hand out of his pocket and showed an automatic pistol apologetically, put it back out of sight.

"That's just by way of clearing up the situation," he said. "By the way, Glastonbury, do you usually go out when some one takes the trouble to pay you a visit?"

Glastonbury's mouth opened and closed soundlessly. Finally he got out words. "Damn you! Damn you!" he shouted, stabbing out an accusing finger. "You said you were coming to the office."

Wentworth raised his tip-tilted brows in raillery. "Nonsense, man," he chided. I asked how late you'd be at the office, that was all."

Glastonbury whirled abruptly, pounded toward a phone. The smile left Wentworth's face. "I wouldn't do that, Glastonbury," he said quietly. His hand was in his gun pocket. The district attorney twisted his head about and stared at him. The Filipino boy came in and put down another glass on the tray with the decanter.

"Pour two drinks," said Wentworth softly. "Easy on the soda."

His eyes never left Glastonbury's face. It paled slowly. He turned awkwardly.

"Won't you join me in a toast, Mr. District Attorney?" asked Wentworth.

Glastonbury moved stiff-legged across the room. Wentworth jerked his head toward the boy and the district attorney said heavily, "That will be all, Cristobal." He moved his arm in a peculiarly stiff gesture. The boy bowed, left hurriedly and the two men faced each other.

"I demand that you surrender your gun," Glastonbury said deliberately, "that you submit to arrest for murder."

Wentworth allowed his lips to smile. "I didn't come here to talk nonsense," he said softly. "I came here to urge you to call at once a conference of all the big food men in the city. Among them somewhere is the man responsible for these fires and the famine of the city."

Glastonbury narrowed prominent eyes, fists locked behind him hunching his shoulders pugnaciously in a characteristic pose. "Surrender first. We'll talk of that later."

Wentworth shook his head. "If I surrendered, the Destroyers never would be captured. They will use the government system to set up a food trust. After this period of terrific prices, goods at twice what it used to cost would seem cheap. Don't you see that this is no coup of a day, or a month, or even of a year? It is a thing planned for years, to continue as long as these criminals can trick the public and escape the penalty.

"Only a man of vast intelligence could have planned it. If you get the food men all in a conference together, I feel positive that you can either get a definite clue to the men, or at least bluff him into being frightened that you know something. He might give himself away somehow."

Glastonbury sneered. "Is that the best you can think up. I've already examined and reexamined every food man in the city, and...."

"But not together," Wentworth thrust in.

"No," Glastonbury conceded. "I haven't done that. There may be something…" abruptly he broke off and grinned, grinned all over his face. "Two of my detectives are behind you, with drawn guns," he said. "Throw your weapon down."

WENTWORTH SMILED. A gruff voice behind repeated the order. "Throw your gun down."

"Certainly," said Wentworth, dipping his hand into his pocket and tossing the second odd-looking pistol he carried to the floor. "It isn't loaded anyhow."

Hands gripped Wentworth's shoulders. Glastonbury, gloating, blew out his chest and strutted toward him. "Thought you could take me in, didn't you. Smart trickster, aren't you? Well, I've had an arrangement with my boy for a long time that when I tell him 'that's all' and move my right hand at the same time, he's to phone headquarters just what's happening in the apartment."

"Very neat," Wentworth complimented him. "I'm sure, I should."

PO-O-WWW!

A pistol blast behind Glastonbury whirled him around, livid-faced. The two police sprang forward, guns tensely ready.

Wentworth smiling, slid a hand into his pocket. From his hip he fired one shot. The light bulb crashed, plunged the room into darkness. Wentworth sat down in his chair beside the decanter, tucked his feet up and waited.

Men pounded about him. Flashlights stabbed about in the dimness of the room. Wentworth's blank pistol with the timing device to fire it, the one which he had tossed to the floor, had succeeded again. He smiled. He felt stimulated by the excitement. He picked up the decanter, weighed it in his hand and sent it flying toward the window a dozen feet away. It made a direct hit, smashed the pane. Pistols blazed bullets toward the casement.

"There he is! At the window!" Glastonbury barked. "Get him!"

A concerted rush of feet pounded toward the window. Wentworth got up deliberately, picked up hat and cane and strolled soft-footed across the room in the opposite direction, slid out into the hall and closed the door softly behind him. He walked up three flights of stairs and rang the elevator bell. Here was no trace of the confusion, thanks to the heavily sound-proofed walls of the expensive apartment house.

The elevator boy took him unsuspiciously to the street. Ram Singh tooled the rented car to the curb. Wentworth, glancing back into the lobby, as he climbed in saw an attendant at a phone gesture excitedly, pointing toward the street. The boy slammed down the phone, pelted toward the door.

The limousine slid forward.

"Better turn off your lights until you've made a few

turns," Wentworth told Ram Singh casually." And head south presently, Ram Singh. We're going to pay a call on Janice Hally at the Marlborough."

CHAPTER 14
THE SPIDER GOES CALLING

WENTWORTH DREW the curtains of the limousine, opened a small suitcase and drew from it the garments of Tito Caliepi. Swiftly he worked and when the car halted, before the Marlborough Hotel, there stepped from it a glorified version of the old virtuoso. His black cloak, graceful even on hunched shoulders, was expensive and the broad brimmed Stetson was jaunty upon long black hair.

Swinging a cane, he strolled into the lobby, and though a conspicuous figure and the cynosure of many eyes, no attendant moved to bar him, even from the ultra ultra Marlborough. He tucked stick beneath his arm, crossed directly to the elevators. Janice Hally was a prisoner on the tenth floor, according to the note he had found in Glastonbury's safe. Wentworth rode to the eighth.

He nodded to the floor clerk and strolled toward where a red light marked the fire stairs. In the Marlborough, as in most modern hotels, there was no fire escape, but a flight of fireproof steps, open to the air on one side and cut off from the main body of the hotel by steel doors. Wentworth opened one of those doors when he had turned a hall corner, noted that it was opposite the room number that corresponded to the girl's, then climbed two flights of stairs to her floor.

But Wentworth did not at once open the fire door into the hall. He twisted the handle of his cane, tugged and unsheathed a sword, hidden in that innocent-seeming stick. He dipped the point in a small vial he took from his pocket, then, sword ready, he warily opened the door a narrow slit. Peering through it, he saw a man pace past the opening and a moment later return. He waited. Once more the man passed and returned like a soldier on sentry duty, paced before Janice Hally's door. Her guard. Wentworth's eyes gleamed. He put the tip of the sword in the slit, then, just as the man was passing, he beat on the door with his fist.

The pacing man whirled toward the fire exit. His hand slid to his hip pocket and the blue steel of a gun glinted. Wentworth knocked again, made muffled sounds like strangled words. The man crept toward him, gun ready at his side. Wentworth watched alertly, sword poised.

The man stretched out his left hand toward the knob of the door and, like a snake striking, the sword flicked through the slit. Its point just touched the hand. It was instantly withdrawn and Wentworth clapped shut the door, gripped the knob and threw his full weight into holding it shut.

Through the door he heard a muffled curse. He felt the man's yank at the door. No need to fear a bullet. Nothing less than an army rifle could pierce that steel. Two, three times, the knob was turned. A fourth time. Wentworth scarcely felt the movement. He smiled thinly, waited another thirty seconds, then thrust open the door.

Janice Hally's guard lay prostrate upon the floor, unconscious. Wentworth caught up the gun, lifted the man and leaned against the door of the girl's room. Probably a matron had been stationed inside, Wentworth thought. He rapped sharply on the panel. Once more the sword was ready in his right hand.

WITHIN WAS no sound. Wentworth rapped again and heard sleepy stirrings. "Hurry up!" he called gruffly.

The voice of a woman who was not Janice Hally snarled at him "Take your time, big boy, take your time. Everything's okay."

"Open up," Wentworth ordered, disguising his voice. "I want to see that everything's okay."

He heard mumbled objections, the heavy stumbling tread of a person half asleep, the door knob rattled and opened.

"What's got into you?" the woman demanded. He saw her bedraggled blonde hair, a sleep-swollen face, a mottled arm?. Once more, Wentworth's sword flicked forward, scratched the arm.

She ripped out a muffled curse. "What the hell's this?"

Wentworth allowed the man to slump forward, pushing open the door.

"For heaven's sake!" he heard the woman exclaim. The words slowed. "Geez, I feel—funny."

Wentworth darted into the room and was in time to catch her as she collapsed. He hauled the man clear out of the door, shut it, switched on the lights. A girl's red hair spilled over the pillow of the bed. As the lights went on, a white arm raised slowly and fell, and a face turned toward him, a sleepy face in which eyes flew abruptly wide and a mouth gaped open. Janice Hally sat bolt upright in bed, a scream starting in her throat, a scream that formed two words, *"The Spider!"*

Wentworth nodded, smiling amicably, and sheathed the narcotic tipped sword into his harmless-seeming cane. He strolled to the side of the bed, leaned both hands upon the stick.

"How are you, Miss Hally? Nice evening."

Fear whitened the girl's face. She clutched the bedclothes to the low neck of her silken gown. "What what do you want?"

Wentworth waved a deprecatory hand. "Just to talk to you, my dear."

"You killed my guards!"

Wentworth shook his head slowly, his eyes never wavering from the girl's. "No, they're just getting a little well-earned sleep. Their relief will not be here for many hours." He thrust forward his beak-nosed face slightly, and his words were soft—"we will not be disturbed."

The girl's face was a rigid mask. Her hands trembled. "Please go away," she begged.

Wentworth raised his brows. "Why so inhospitable, Miss Hally? You are scarcely gracious."

"Please!" the girl implored.

Wentworth's smile faded. "Enough of this," he said. "I've something serious to say to you. You are hostile to me, as I understand it, because you believe I am implicated in the apparent death of your sweetheart. The reasons your suspicions attach to me, I do not know. But I am here to assure you that

121

I am not guilty of that or of these fires the Destroyers set. But these charges I do not mind. I want you to withdraw the false affidavit against Miss Van Sloan."

The girl's trembling increased. "I can't!"

"You mean you would not be allowed?"

The girl jerked her head in affirmative.

Wentworth leaned more heavily upon his cane. His face thrust closer to the girl's. "That also," he said, "is why I am here, to take you away so that you can be free to withdraw those affidavits."

The girl inched backward until she crowded her body against the head of the bed. "No," she shook her head violently. "No, I won't go with you."

WENTWORTH'S LIPS began slowly to lift. The smile did not extend to his eyes, and the wax-distorted face he had assumed was an evil thing. "I cannot blame you," he said, "for fearing the Spider. But in this case, I give my word that as soon as you reach the street you shall be free."

The girl stared. "You mean that?"

"My dear, apparently you do not know the Spider. Wherever he is known in the Underworld, it is known that when he gives his word, he keeps it."

Still staring at him, the girl swung her feet to the floor, drew the covers around her as a cloak, and fled into the bath.

Wentworth backed across the room. A mocking smile on his lips, he laid the two unconscious police guards side by side on the floor, folded their hands upon their chests and placed artificial flowers from a vase in their hands. Beside the scratch of his sword point, he imprinted the seal of the Spider.

"Something for Glastonbury to wonder about," he chuckled to himself, as he opened the door and slid across the hall to the fire exit. He slipped through and closed the metal door except for a slit from which he could watch Janice Hally's room.

In less than ten minutes, the door opened and the girl, a felt hat dragged down over red hair, peered down the hall. Her eyes narrowed suspiciously, but she stepped boldly out of the room, shut the door and walked openly down the hall.

Wentworth smiled quietly and closed his door. Deliberately he descended two flights, peered as before from the slit and, finding no one in sight, walked to the elevators, through the lobby. At the door, he caught a taxi, giving a Park Avenue address. His swift glance about showed that Ram Singh and the limousine had disappeared on the trail of Janice Hally, If only she would lead him to some hide-out of the Food Destroyers, he might uncover some clue to the leaders. It was a dim trail, but it constituted his chief hope.

Wentworth leaned back comfortably and watched taxis rush past along Central Park South, grinned irresistibly as his own driver muscled in ahead of a lounging Rolls Royce and charged a changing traffic light at Fifth Avenue, with a net gain of three seconds.

The Spider hoped, yawning and tapping thin white fingers across his mouth, that Xavier Jones would be at home, would not keep him, Tito Caliepi, waiting.

THE TAXI whirled north on Park Avenue. Swerving to the

curb, it forced a Lincoln to squeal brakes to prevent a collision, and the driver kicked open the door with the heel of his hand. Wentworth descended gravely and paid the meter.

He smiled and strolled, cane swinging, down the Avenue, only the hunched shoulder marring the elegant figure of the old maestro, black cloak swaying with the broken rhythm of his walking. But here he could not approach openly. He wanted to surprise Jones alone and in view of the fact that Jones had been threatened, he would certainly have guards in and about his home.

But for the Spider, that presented few obstacles. He turned openly into the tradesman's entrance of Xavier Jones' apartment, used a lock pick on the basement door and found the dumb waiter, which served the vacant penthouse on the same floor with Jones. Ensconcing himself on its top, he began leisurely the long trip upward, hauling on the rope, hand over hand.

At long last, he reached the penthouse, went through it to the roof. He crossed rapidly then to Jones' side of the building and peered downward. Below him yawned twenty stories, two hundred feet and more of black space. The terrace was off to his left. Wentworth's keen eyes studied it. A chair rested in the shadows and it was occupied. Wentworth crouched low, watching, and presently a man got up, stretched and moved reluctantly toward the house, obviously one of the guards. No entrance there.

Wentworth returned to the sheer wall, glanced along the rampart. A ventilator pipe caught his eye and he nodded, leaned out and scanned the wall. He located a window with frosted glass, a bath. Next to that would be a bedroom. The bath would offer the safer entrance.

From the compact tool kit beneath his arm, he drew the slender silken cord which many times had served him in his need, a silken cord that seemed scarcely able to support the weight of a cat, yet which tested at seven hundred pounds. He noosed it about the ventilator pipe, tested cord, knot and pipe with violent tugs, then straddled the wall and twisted the cord tightly around a leg and arm. It was too small to grasp with the hands.

Wentworth took two turns around his other arm with the cord and lowered himself over the depths. A chill wind whispered along the wall. Autos on the streets below were crawling beetles, with beams of light for antennae. Men were dots. Wentworth's mouth twisted. If anything went wrong with the rope or his grip, there would be a slightly larger dot spread upon the pavement below.

The silken cord bit into his arms and leg through his clothing. He let it slip inch by inch, relaxing the friction on one arm by pointing it straight up the cord. By twisting his arm at right angles, he could check his descent. The black wall slid up past his eyes. The playful wind tugged at his coat and swayed him slightly. Wentworth's knees scraped the bricks.

Lower he slipped. Without warning, he felt the cord give a full inch. His body dropped, checked sharply. His breath caught in his throat. Wentworth jerked his arm at right angles to halt his descent, felt the cord give again. Either the ventilator pipe was pulling loose or the knot was slipping! Below yawned a black chasm of death.

Wentworth pointed his arm straight up the cord, allowed himself to slip rapidly downward. His knees dropped below the window top. The cord sagged again. Wentworth's jaw was locked grimly. Two more feet he slid with increasing speed, then, deliberately, he twisted the arm he used as a brake free of the cord, slapped his hand downward and smashed his fist through the window glass, seized hold of the sash. In the same instant, the cord came loose entirely. Wentworth shot downward. His toes caught at the window sill, his weight surged outward against that one hand. One hand's grip between him and death. His toes slipped. His body fell full length, beat against the wall.

Dangling by one hand, a hand gashed by broken glass, Wentworth swung out over the chasm of death. Frantically he strained upward with his other hand, the wound-weakened left arm, and caught hold of the sash. Strangely no alarm had been sounded within. There was no help save in himself. He rested a moment, then attempted to flex his arms, drawing his weight upward. One inch, two inches he gained, then his muscles gave out. He sagged at arm's length again. That month of illness had sapped his strength. Numbness began to steal from his aching fingers up his arms.

CHAPTER 15
A ONE-WAY TRAP

H E CLUNG panting. But there was no time to rest. The moments his hands would hold were numbered. He twisted his left knee upward, pressing its scraped flesh harshly against the bricks. Cautiously he rolled back and put his weight upon that knee. It put more strain on his hands. Aching pain surged up his arms. But it was now or never. And he must hurry, hurry.

He inched his other knee upward. By forcing his body out from the wall, he raised his shoulders. Throwing all the strain for an instant upon his slashed and weakening right hand, he pulled his shoulders inward, sliding his left arm through the break, got his knees upon the sill—at last! He eased to a kneeling position. His breath hissed between clenched teeth. He closed his eyes while strength flowed back into his weakened body.

Another sound rose even above the labor of his breath, the sound of rushing water within. He understood now why the tinkle of breaking glass had not been heard. In a darkened bathroom, someone was drawing a tub of water.

That had drowned out the noise. But the tub must be nearly full. Any instant now, the occupant of the bedroom would enter and find him clinging to the sill, an easy capture for the guards, steadying himself gingerly, he turned the latch of the window and contrived to inch up the lower sash and climb in. He leaned against the wall panting. His knees were trembling with fatigue, but a slight smile lifted his tight-drawn lips. Well, the professor had advised him to take it easy.... Wentworth snaked a gun from his pocket, stole toward the bathroom door and peered into the dimly lighted bedroom. A gaunt man in a bathrobe, was seated on the side of a bed, his back turned toward the door, and scanning a newspaper.

Wentworth caught up his sword cane, which he had swung from the back of his belt, thrust its glinting gray steel ahead of him. He dropped his gun into his pocket and stole into the room, completely steadied now by the need for action. The sword would be more terrifying than the pistol. And if he were forced to quiet Jones, a touch of the narcotic-dipped point would account for him in a few seconds.

Wentworth stepped against the opposite side of the bed, leveled the sword cane.

"Not a word, Jones, not a sound," he said quietly.

The gaunt figure of the man stiffened. His head came up slowly and he stared into a mirror on the wall ahead of him. Wentworth permitted his distorted face to grin, evilly. Xavier Jones' mouth fell open, then clicked shut. He jerked to his feet, whirled around. Wentworth leaned forward slightly and presented the point of the sword to Jones' exposed and hair-matted chest.

"That's fine," he said softly. "Now lie down on the bed and turn out the light. You and I are going to have a little talk."

"Who—who are you?" Jones got out drily, his voice croaking. "What do you want?"

"I want to have a little talk," Wentworth repeated. "As to

who I am—" once more the slow, evil grin—"I will tell you this. If I am forced to kill you, I will print on your forehead a little red seal shaped like a spider."

JONES CHOKED back the scream that bubbled into his throat. His arms were stiff as pokers.

Wentworth's sword arm straightened so that the blade moved a quarter inch nearer Jones' chest. "Lie down."

Awkwardly Jones put a knee on the bed, eased down with the sword point hovering near. He reached out a gaunt arm for the light and in the instant the lamp went out, the white beam from Wentworth's hand torch struck him full in the eyes. He stood by the bed with the sword ready. "Now we can talk," he said. "What do you know about the Food Destroyers?"

In the white beam, Jones' face was pasty. "N—Nothing," he said.

"Come, come," said Wentworth impatiently. "I'm not a friend of the Destroyers, you know. I'm their enemy. I'm asking for information."

"But, I don't know anything," Jones insisted, nodding his long, thin checked head on the pillow. "I've been threatened by them. I've…" He broke off, eyes glinting hopefully.

"I know you've got guards here," Wentworth assured him. "But you're not going to be able to trap me with them. Go ahead."

Jones seemed to sink deeper into the fear which gripped him. "Yes, I have guards," he admitted slowly. "But that's all I know. Glastonbury has questioned me. He's called me into a meeting at the Waldorf tomorrow for more questioning."

"What room?"

Jones stared at Wentworth without comprehension for a moment and he was forced to repeat the question before Jones told him. Satisfaction gleamed in Wentworth's eyes. The district attorney had lost no time in summoning the conference the Spider had advised.

"I'm afraid even to go to that," Jones said, "for fear these dastardly murderers will get me on the street."

"Then don't go," Wentworth advised softly. "I'll fix it up with Glastonbury."

"You'll…?"

Wentworth nodded. "Don't puzzle yourself about how. It will be done." He leaned forward. "I'll tell you something else. Over a month ago, a bomb thrower was hiding in the vacant apartment across the hall to kill you and I drove him out. I tell you this to give you confidence in me. Now tell me what you know about the gang and its workings."

"But I tell you…" Jones' voice rose querulously.

A knock at the door choked his voice. Wentworth crowded the sword point against his neck. "Silence," he ordered. He waited. The knock was repeated.

"Who's that?" he demanded, imitating Jones' booming grave tones.

"The police!" A man called back. "The Spider was seen entering this building. We're going to search your rooms for him!"

A slow smile spread over Jones' face. Wentworth's eyes darted about the room. No place of concealment, no retreat. The silken escape to the roof was gone.

"Open up," the voice ordered impatiently, "or we'll smash the door. You've got one minute."

One minute to wait, one to smash the door. What could the Spider do in two minutes to escape from a bare room whose only exits were windows opening on twenty stories of empty space, and a door at which police pounded?

Jones' grin widened.

CHAPTER 16
A DISGUISE FAILS

XAVIER JONES' smile at Wentworth's predicament became a smirk of triumph.

"You are trapped very prettily," he gloated. "You haven't a chance to escape."

Wentworth did not answer with words, but a slow smile spread over his disguised features. His sword point was still at Jones' throat. He pricked the flesh, watched Jones thresh his arms frantically on the bed, Jones' eyes were wide in fear.

Wentworth lifted his voice in booming imitation of Jones. "I don't care to be disturbed," he called irascibly. "There's nobody in here except myself."

He watched Jones closely, saw him move his tongue drily, saw his pupils dilate. Still smiling, Wentworth removed his sword, thrust it into the cane sheath. Jones tossed his head, tried to mouth words. He thrust his arms against the bed to raise himself. Abruptly, animation went out of his body. He dropped

down limply, completely under the influence of the narcotic with which Wentworth had tipped his sword.

Hurriedly Wentworth stripped the bathrobe from him. Fists pounded on the door again. "I'm sorry, Mr. Jones, you'll have to open up. Our orders are to search every room."

"Nonsense!" Wentworth boomed, thrusting his own cloak and hat under the bed, drawing on the bathrobe. "I refuse to be disturbed! You have no right—I'll see the commissioner!"

The gruff voice beyond the door interrupted him again de-

Brilliant yellow and
red flame shot upward
enveloping the man.

manding entrance. Wentworth crouched before a mirror, drew
out his emergency make-up kit and laid it before him on a chest
of drawers. He paused, daubing on shadow paint to make his
jaws seem sunken, worked frantically on his face, glancing

swiftly now and again at Jones. The wig of Tito Caliepi was perfect for the disguise.

"I'm sorry, sir," the voice called again. "Our orders are definite. If you don't open within ten seconds we shall break down the door."

He straightened, inspecting himself in the mirror, turned and studied Jones. Side by side, he might not pass scrutiny, but seen alone—Wentworth twisted his lips in imitation of the other's dour grin, drew himself up stiffly. He rolled Jones to a position where the bed clothes, tossed back as if a man had just sprung from bed, would cover him. He turned his head to the side and laid a pillow against his cheek.

"Ten seconds up," the voice warned outside. "Are you going to open?"

"You bet I will." Wentworth bellowed, "and you'll be sorry for it!"

He hit his feet heavily on the floor, flung open the door and stalked into the adjoining room.

He confronted three men in police uniform, two others obviously were Jones' guards. Two of the police whirled and ran, the third jerked his hand from beneath his tunic. Wentworth flung himself aside, snapped a pistol from his pocket and fired before the man in uniform could hurl the gleaming glass cylinder he clutched.

Wentworth's bullet smashed through the cylinder. The uniformed man screamed, staggered backward. Liquid spilled from the glass cylinder. As it splashed toward the floor, drenching the uniform, it turned into liquid flame. Brilliant yellow and red tongues shot upward, enveloped the man. Spots of fire blossomed on the rug.

WENTWORTH PLUNGED back into the bedroom, crouched with only his head exposed, but the other two in uniform had fled precipitately. The guards shrank back from the flame-enveloped man on the floor. Screams tore from him.

Wentworth's bullet had crashed through the glass, buried itself in his body, but torture of the blaze spurred him to his feet. A living torch, he plunged blindly across the room. He struck a wall, caromed aside, raced on. Hangings ignited from his body. The guards leaped at those, tore them down and tramped them out.

A door slammed. The screams became remote, then died. Wentworth came slowly into the room, stamped out the last flames upon the charred rug. One of the guards turned from extinguishing a drapery. He was a heavily-built man who walked alertly on his toes, like a boxer. He came toward Wentworth shaking a heavy head that seemed to spring neckless directly from his shoulders.

"Jeez!" he exclaimed, "that was some shot. Mr. Jones. I didn't even know you packed a rod."

Wentworth nodded gravely in imitation of Jones' stiffness. "It was largely luck," he said heavily.

"Some luck," said the guard. He was within two yards of Wentworth now and he stood balanced on his toes and surveyed him curiously. "Seems to me you said you didn't even like firearms."

Wentworth stiffened. He stared at the man haughtily. "Just what are you driving at?" he demanded.

"Nothing at all, nothing at all," the guard muttered, He looked down at Wentworth's feet. The man's partner, a short wiry man with a face as thin as a cheese knife, strode alertly into the room.

"He's corked," he announced briskly. "I called the cops."

He stopped short at seeing the strained stance of the two men in the room, and then glanced swiftly from Wentworth to his bulky partner. He kept on talking cheerfully, but his small eyes flicked about the room.

"Swell job you did, Mr. Jones. Could not have done better myself!"

"That's just what I was saying," his heavier partner said softly. He stared at Wentworth's feet again, and the smaller guard's eyes followed his. Wentworth's narrowed gaze spotted an almost imperceptible start. Hell, he had overlooked some point of disguise. Possibly one of Jones' feet was twisted. He spun toward the bedroom, hesitated, then strode across the room past the two.

"Call me when the police come," he ordered brusquely.

"Hold on, *Mr. Jones*," the burly guard drawled, "I want...."

Wentworth glimpsed his reflection in a picture glass, a gun in his hand. He was only two feet away. Without pausing in his stride, Wentworth pivoted on his right heel, crashed his left fist into the guard's jaw. The guard spilled against his smaller partner. Wentworth snatched the man's gun, leveled it and his own, one in each fist. A frigid twist of his lips was a mocking smile.

The larger guard was crouched, small murderous eyes redly on Wentworth, but he made no effort to charge the guns.

"You, Shorty, get your partner's handcuffs and snap them on him," Wentworth ordered softly. "Remember, these two guns can shoot two men at once… and I'm a pretty fair shot."

The two men snarled, but finally Wentworth had them handcuffed with their own manacles. He stripped adhesive across their mouths and locked them in a closet. He started for Jones' bedroom to recover the cane and cloak. A fist pounded at the door.

Wentworth frowned, but did not hesitate. He strode to the door, glanced through a small, round peephole in its middle and saw men in uniform, with them was the suave, elegant form of Stanley Kirkpatrick, commissioner of police. Too late to stall now.

Wentworth fumbled with the locks. With his left hand he extracted a small rugged file from the kit beneath his arm. He concealed it in his hand, flung wide the door.

"Glad you came, Commissioner," he boomed in Jones' grave voice. "It was positively terrifying, and those two rascally guards of mine have run away."

Kirkpatrick's voice crashed out a sharp command. "Arrest that man," he snapped out and pointed at Wentworth.

THE MOUTH of the false Jones sagged open, then clicked shut. He drew himself up stiffly, "explain yourself, sir," he said angrily, "or the mayor…."

Kirkpatrick re-iterated his order and smiled when two police swung on to Wentworth's arms. He touched a thumbnail to his black, pointed mustache. "You say your two guards ran away? They were two of my most trusted men; they wouldn't leave before seeing me. And you recognize me. Jones never saw me in his life.

"Obviously you are an impostor, though who you are I do not know. Search the entire apartment immediately," he ordered the other police. "Two of our men are prisoners here." He faced Wentworth again. "If you care to tell me where they are, it will save time… and perhaps be easier for you."

Wentworth's thoughts were racing madly. Kirkpatrick's cleverness had penetrated the subterfuge all too readily, though he doubted if his identity was known. The removal of his disguise, however, would accomplish that and connect him to that cane with its narcotic point. And that, in turn, would implicate him in the escape of Janice Halley.

Whether it invoked him in the depredations of the Flame Men or not, he would be forced out of the war against the Food Destroyers. And just at a time when the battle was coming to a crisis, just when he had laid his plans to trace the leader of the gang and strike a damaging blow!

He could not submit to arrest. Yet with two police and the commissioner watching him, how could he escape?

"Search him," Kirkpatrick ordered brusquely, and two guns, his own and the one taken from the guard, were revealed. The commissioner instantly identified the latter. His face went grim, his lips compressed angrily.

"All right, all right," said Wentworth, "I'll show you where your men are."

He turned toward the doorway, the two cops still gripping his arms. He went through first, lurched to one side, grinding one of those pinioning hands against the door jamb. The cop cursed, jerked his hand away. Wentworth caught the door, slammed it in the face of the other. In the same instant he jammed the file he had concealed in his hand into the closing crack.

A gun blazed outside, but Wentworth had thrown himself aside. Shoulders thumped against the door. From distantly within the apartment, startled shouts of the searching cops rang out in answer.

WENTWORTH DARTED down the hall. He ducked into the kitchen just in time to escape being seen as a cop rushed down the hall to open the door. The file would wedge it tight and thwart that, too. Wentworth bounded to the dumbwaiter, jerked it open and flung himself inside. Grabbing the rope, he let himself down rapidly.

As he descended, sounds of music and shouting reached him. He opened the shaft door a crack. The kitchen was empty and drunken singing, cries of hilarity came from the next room.

Wentworth sprang into the kitchen, jerked off the bathrobe and wig and tossed them down an incinerator shaft. With swift hands, he swept make-up from his face, leaving only the mis-shapen nose of Jones. He wadded putty back of his ears to make them fan out from his head, then he slipped out the kitchen door of the apartment. He went rapidly to the front door and rang the bell. It took five efforts to get somebody to the door.

A man in a drink-stained tuxedo and a girl, whose long

blonde hair streamed over her shoulders, opened the door. They had an arm about each other and they swayed, grinning at him tipsily. Wentworth smiled back.

"Say," he said, "I don't like to be a crab about parties, but I been trying to sleep for hours without any luck at all. How about me joining the party?"

The man's smile expanded. He reached out his other arm for Wentworth's shoulders, clasped him into a warm and hiccoughy embrace with the girl.

"A man," he declaimed, "a man after my own-hic-heart."

Wentworth came inside and joined the party.

Presently he was able to improve on his makeup. He suggested that they dress in one another's clothes and the idea was hilariously greeted. When police came hunting him, Wentworth had on a fluffy blue negligee and a dust cap and drunkenly pressed drinks upon the two cops. They accepted a couple each and went out grinning.

Wentworth laughed, and reeled off. Once in the kitchen, he became completely sober. Eyes narrowed intently, he hauled himself back up the dumbwaiter shaft to Jones' apartment.

CHAPTER 17
THE RED COUNCIL

AT THE head of the shaft, Wentworth listened for a long time for movement within Xavier Jones' apartment. Finally, he eased open the dumbwaiter door and climbed out. He moved on soundless feet through the unlighted kitchen toward the drawing room where a soft lamp glowed.

Peering from behind a hall portière, he stopped rigidly, holding his breath. A woman sat upon the luxurious divan that angled across the room before a stone fireplace. She was dressed in the starched white of a nurse and, her head lolling back, she was asleep. A slow smile lifted Wentworth's lips. He slid a hand to the narcotic vial beneath his arm, tipped a pin with it and, on hands and knees, crept up behind the sleeping woman.

He pricked the back of her neck with the pin. She started in her sleep, mumbled, subsided. Her deep breathing resumed. Wentworth glanced in at Jones and saw that he still slept peacefully. Then, fishing the hat, cloak and cane of Tito Caliepi from beneath the bed, he went swiftly to a phone. He called Ram Singh at a pre-arranged number. The Hindu's alert voice responded promptly.

In silence, Wentworth heard the report of Janice Hally's movements, of her going to a speakeasy and making three phone calls. Wentworth repeated these, penciling on a notebook as Ram Singh gave them, glanced at-the number of the instrument he held. Ram Singh then gave him the location of the girl's present quarters.

"Fine," Wentworth said briefly. "Stay at that phone until I call again."

He hung up and pivoted, staring past the gently snoring nurse toward the door behind which Xavier Jones slept. He strode to the room and got out his makeup kit. He slid into place the celluloid canine teeth which made his grinning mouth

Wentworth dropped to the floor;
both guns spoke together.

so hideous. Bit by bit he resumed the full disguise of Tito Caliepi, whom the flame gang knew now as the Spider.

Extracting a hypodermic needle, he made an injection in Jones' throat. He waited five minutes and made another. Jones stirred, moved his arms restlessly, fluttered his eyes.

The room was in darkness except for a small lamp which glared like a spotlight on the evil, grinning face of the beak-nosed man with teeth like a wolf; a sallow, thin-jawed countenance framed in drooping black hair.

Wentworth spoke softly: "The Spider has come for the reckoning!"

Xavier Jones moved stiffly on the bed. He tossed his head. "Stop that tomfoolery," he muttered thickly.

Wentworth struck his hand heavily across Jones' face. The man's eyes flew wide. Terror seeped into them. "You feared me earlier today," Wentworth told him, "because you thought I came from the Food Destroyers. After I put you to sleep, their assassins came. They were those who posed as police and demanded entrance. I disguised myself as you and they tried to kill me. I killed one of them instead."

Wentworth paused and watched Jones' eyes darken with fright, watched him lick dry lips that trembled. He leaned closer, his lips barely moving: "How is it that you, a member of the food syndicate, face death at the hands of his friends?"

Jones rolled his head from side to side on the pillow. "They are not my friends!"

Wentworth lips twisted from the pointed, gleaming teeth. Jones shuddered, flung a forearm across his eyes.

"Janice Hally phoned a little while ago," said Wentworth, quietly.

Jones jerked his arm from his face, and stared wild-eyed.

"She thought I was you," the Spider went on, "due possibly to the fact that I made my voice sound like yours."

"Who—who is Janice Hally?" Jones asked. Wentworth laughed. It was sibilant, almost silent laughter, but it was mirthful.

JONES' FACE grew white. "In God's name," he cried, "what do you want with me?"

Wentworth continued to laugh. He checked abruptly, stared stonily into Jones' eyes. "Have you told Janice Hally the truth about Hanford Tyson's death?" he demanded.

Shuddering breath sucked between Jones' teeth. He closed his eyes.

"You see," said Wentworth, "I know everything. You might as well talk. It might help you some when this case goes to trial."

Jones' head rolled again on the hard-packed pillow. "No," he groaned hoarsely, "No. My life is forfeit, but, so help me God, the deaths were none of my planning! It was because I fought those needless murders that I was doomed." He opened his eyes wide, peered up into Wentworth's face. "I want you to believe that. You are that mysterious avenger who calls himself the Spider. If you avenge the thousands who have been killed, let one of your blows be for me. For I, too, shall die!"

Wentworth nodded slowly. He did not speak.

"I don't know how much you know—" Jones began and hesitated. Then as Wentworth maintained his silence, went on swiftly. "I went into a food syndicate as a business venture. The plan was to control production, carry further the government's plan for the farmers by cutting the supplies so as to lift prices. It sounded legitimate enough. I contributed money. When I learned the real purpose behind the thing, my associates threatened me with exposure if I spoke."

Jones closed his eyes slowly. His gaunt face worked as if to force back tears that threatened. He swallowed loudly, went on: "I still did not realize the full enormity of the crimes. When I did I was doomed, and for weeks now I have fought off death only by remaining inside my home. Today, they penetrated even here."

"Who were your associates?" Wentworth asked.

Jones shook his heavy head. "I do not know."

"What!"

Jones shook his head again. "At the meetings we all wear red hoods. It was supposed to be protection from rival spies at the first meetings. Later I understood."

"Where do you meet?"

"In a hotel, a different room usually. There's a notice in my coat pocket of a meeting tomorrow." Jones spoke like an automaton. There was no animation in his voice, none in his face except those burning, haunted eyes.

"And Hanford Tyson?" Wentworth's voice was soft.

A strong shudder shook Jones' body. "I can't talk about that."

"But you must!"

Jones eyes swung up to Wentworth's, met their had commanding gaze. He fumbled with the covers and dragged them aside. He pressed a hand to his forehead.

"I feel… I want some water," he mumbled and walked heavy-footed into the bath. Wentworth heard water turned on. He stood staring into blackness. A meeting in a hotel tomorrow! His eyes narrowed.

He stepped to Jones' neatly hung clothing, groped in the pockets and found a card. "Room 317, the Dorfawl." Date and time, "10 a.m." were printed upon it. Wentworth clenched it in his hand. The sound of a fall whirled him toward the bath. He plunged in, jerked to a halt, staring at the floor.

Jones was stretched out in a welter of blood. He had gashed his throat with a dagger of glass from the broken window. For frantic moments, Wentworth worked over him, but the man had been dead almost before he fell.

WENTWORTH STOOD erect, white lines about tight-pressed lips. One of the Food Destroyers had paid the penalty. One life to pay for thousands, one life while the others still sent their fiery death stalking over the earth.

He shut the door on Jones' death, swiftly began to strip off the disguise of the Spider. He rapidly became again Xavier Jones. He dressed completely in the dead man's clothes and then discovered how he had been detected by the guards. The man wore an abnormally high heel on the right foot to equalize a shortened leg. He hunted for and finally found a crimson hood.

The disguise perfected, he packed the garments of the Spider in a small portfolio and walked out past the snoring nurse. He made a phone call to Ram Singh, opened the door and looked into the face of a policeman with a drawn gun!

For an instant Wentworth's muscles tightened, then he smiled dourly and jerked his head in a nod.

"If you're guarding me," he said shortly, "come to the Dorfawl Hotel. I don't think this place is safe any longer."

The policeman thrust his gun away. "Sure," he said, "my orders are to guard you and I'd just as soon do it at the Dorfawl as here."

Wentworth nodded stiffly, the elevator. The two men went by taxi to the hotel. There Wentworth testily demanded room 418. He finally compromised on 420 and, reaching that room and placing the policeman on guard outside, phoned Ram Singh again. That done, he threw himself upon the bed and promptly went to sleep.

Next morning at the time named on Jones' card, Wentworth went to 317. He knocked, was spied on through the peephole, then admitted. As he entered, he donned the red hood, stared stiffly about him. There were four other men in red hoods grouped together in a corner. Their eyes through slits regarded him fixedly. Two men wore black masks. They tended the door. Wentworth did not approach the others. Jones had been a silent, unsociable man.

As if Wentworth's entrance had been a signal, a constant line of others arrived until twenty red-masked figures stood silently like soldiers on parade, no man speaking to his neighbor. A door in the side wall opened and the red-masked man nearest it strode through it. After seconds of silence, the door opened again. The next man entered. The routine went on.

Wentworth waited with thumping pulses. It was obvious that beyond that door some sort of identification was made. If there were a secret formula to be given, or any definite thing to be done, he would have to bluff through it on the strength of his disguise.

He waited in complete surface calm, his eyes not even fixed

on the doorway, but his pulses were thumping. There was a gun beneath each arm. The man next to Wentworth stalked through the door. The eyes of the room swung automatically to Wentworth as the door opened again. He walked austerely toward it, with Jones slight limp on his high-heeled shoe.

The room beyond the door was a bath. In it stood a man who stared at Wentworth impassively through the slits of a red mask. He was a bulky, broad man in formal morning clothes. Wentworth jerked off the red velvet that covered his head.

"I warn you," he said stiffly, "that I am going to demand an explanation for that attempt to kill me. I won't be persecuted!"

A dry voice issued from behind the other mask: "That is your privilege, of course, Jones. I thought I recognized you." The figure jerked its head toward the door beyond and Wentworth, drawing the mask on again, stalked through it. A long table gleamed in the middle of the room. On each side were seated the red masks. Wentworth went gravely to the vacant seat. He leaned back stiffly in his chair and stared straight ahead of him. THE SUMMARY went on. Man after man drifted in until all seats except that at the head of the table were filled. Finally that, too, was taken, without ceremony by the stocky man who had confronted them all in the team. He sat, eyeing them individually.

"Tonight we strike again," he began without preamble. He spoke heavily, in dry precise, syllables as if he read a treasurers report. "It will be necessary to use a decoy, because of the perfected fire defense system developed by Commissioner Kirkpatrick. But these are minor details. You were called to determine whether the time was at hand when Washington must be taken over. I want you to think of that while the fiscal report is read."

The man at his right began to reel off figures in a monotone. They ran into the millions, the profits of the Food Destroyers. Wentworth clenched his fists beneath the level of the table, waiting.

He saw each sheet of the report burned as it was read on a silver tray on the table. The chairman ground the ashes with a spoon. The last page raised its thin wisp of smoke and blackened, became pulverized ash.

The stocky man at the head of the table turned his direct gaze upon Wentworth. The eyes were shadowed but showed gleaming, small and hostile.

"You have something to say?"

Wentworth stood his full gaunt height. "I have," he said flatly. He slowly pulled off his mask. It rumpled his lank hair. Spires of it thrust out sticky from his head, incongruous with the sombre gravity of his face. He met each slitted gaze about the table, then turned to the glittering venomous of the leader's. He spoke deliberately.

"Yesterday an attempt was made to assassinate me with a fire bomb. I demand an explanation!"

Masked heads leaned together. The leader rose. He was not so tall as Wentworth, but his width was greater. His hands, gripping the table edge, were pink and white from pressure. He waited for silence. Wentworth remained standing also. Their eyes clashed. Wentworth gave him no opportunity to speak.

"That order to kill me was issued by you personally," he rasped, his voice the booming bass of Jones. "It is obvious the council knows nothing of it. Are you plotting to kill us all one by one, and then rule alone?"

No whispers answered that charge. Men sat rigidly, eyes shuttling from one to the other of the standing men. The leader struck his palm on the table. "You are a traitor. The penalty is death," he delivered heavily.

"Your accusation is sufficient to convict me, I suppose?" Wentworth's voice dripped sarcasm. "You did not need to consult the council on so small a matter as the murder of one of its members?"

The leader jerked his hand from the table as if it were hot. It clenched at his side. Wentworth felt his heart pounding hard and slowly, high in his chest. He had come to this meeting with a threefold purpose: to learn its plans, to capture its members, to spread dissension. If he accomplished any one of those the Spider could triumph.

Wentworth turned from the leader, swung his arm in a stiff gesture. "Suppose the judgment had been passed on you?" He pointed toward a red-masked head. "Or you? Do you want this man to sit in single judgment on whether you shall live or die? I tell you, he plots to rule alone!"

"A nice speech," the leader cut in, his voice edged. "But it happens there were witnesses to your disaffection."

Wentworth spun toward him. "I thought I was a traitor?" he exclaimed. "Now the crime is something else."

"You told me in the presence of witnesses," the leader pushed on, each word emphatic, "that you would have no further part in the fires, that you considered us a gang of—I think I quote your precise words—'cold-blooded slaughter brokers.' Knowing how weak-kneed men of your stamp are in a crisis, I ordered your execution lest you succumb to conscience and go to the police with your knowledge."

THE LEADER appealed to the council now. He swung his hand in a choppy, inclusive gesture. "If anyone of you did that, you would expect death. I tell you the thing was done for the protection of all of us. This man"—his finger stabbed at Wentworth—"is a menace to each of you personally. If a sore threatens to turn cancerous, do you wait for the cancer to develop to cut it out? When a man turns weak, shall we wait for him to go to the police, before we silence him?"

A mutter rose from the red masks.

"You say there are witnesses," Wentworth bit out. Produce them."

A man directly opposite Wentworth stood. Another at the foot of the table rose. The leader faced Wentworth. "These are my witnesses."

"Bah," snarled Wentworth, They're as anonymous as unsigned letters. Take off the masks."

There was hesitancy. The two standing men looked to the leader. He jerked his head in a nod and the masks were stripped off instantly. Wentworth stared at the two. One was Callahan, the humor gone from his heavy, blond face. The other was a wealthy coffee man Wentworth knew.

"Are you two prepared to swear to this lie he tells?" Wentworth demanded. Callahan flushed, his small blue eyes glinting.

"It's the truth. You're as yellow as gold. If he doesn't order you killed, I'll do the job myself."

"So you're in on the plot, too, Callahan? The plot to seize all the wealth for yourself?" Wentworth demanded.

It was a shrewd blow but even as he struck it, he knew he had failed. The council was convinced. A trick of personality did it. Callahan was liked. Jones wasn't. They wanted to believe Callahan. The leader was quick to sense the shift.

"I demand the execution of this traitor," he snapped. "Is it the sense of this council that Jones should die?"

A mutter rose from the red masks. The mutter said "Yes."

Wentworth whirled and found two black-masked men behind him with leveled guns. He turned slowly back to the table, facing the council. They would not shoot him here, in the hotel, he was sure. For the moment he was safe.

Wentworth drew down the wide mouth of Jones in a sneer. "Do you think I came unprepared for such a decision?" He demanded. "Do you think that my mere death can hide the things I know?"

Once more heads were bunched and whispering, but the leader was unmoved. "Any accusation you can make through papers will come too late to affect us." He raised a clenched, powerful fist. "From tonight on, we rule!"

A BUZZER rasped in the waiting silence that followed his words and the leader started, moved a hand in signal to one of the black-masked guards. He crossed to the door, admitted another black mask who hurried to the leader's side.

"Report to the council," the leader ordered shortly.

The man turned to the red masks which centered on him. "I was sent this morning to remove Xavier Jones. I found him dead, his throat cut, in the bathroom of his apartment."

His eyes spotted Wentworth, and his sharp intake of breath was audible throughout the room.

"You are *sure?*" the leader asked softly.

He was looking not at the assassin, but at Wentworth. All other faces swung to him. Wentworth was conscious of the gunmen drawing nearer with leveled weapons. Beneath his makeup the thin line of a white scar throbbed on his right temple. He looked slowly over the hooded figures before him, a slight smile on his disguised face. Death glared at him through the slits of twenty red masks.

"I rather thought my little subterfuge would be discovered," Wentworth said calmly in his normal tone of voice, "but it's too late to help you." As if it were an answer to his words, the door jerked open and a man yelled: "The hall's full of cops!"

Wentworth continued to smile. "Yes, I expect it is," he said.

Men's hands gripped Wentworth's shoulders, the hands of the black-masked gunmen.

"Quick, the escape door!" the leader barked.

Another black-masked man darted to the wall, paneled high in wood. He ran his hand along the molding and a door opened into the next room. Swiftly, silently, the red-masked men filed through it. From the ante-room of the chamber came the sound of thunderous blows on wood.

The leader reached the door, turned. "Kill him, and follow us!" he spat.

Wentworth dropped to the floor, hands whipping beneath his arms. He rolled, and both guns spoke together. Two bullets ploughed the table where Wentworth had stood a moment before. Two men in black masks wavered. One reeled to the wall; the other crumpled forward. Wentworth sprang to his knees, both his guns ready. The secret door snapped shut behind the leader.

Wentworth delayed a moment longer. He printed on the black-masked faces of the two he had slain the small red seal of the Spider, then skipped across to the secret panel and marked that, too. If the police used their heads, they would know what that meant.

There was a splintering crash from the adjoining room. The door smashed in. Wentworth ran to the window, threw it up, leaped to the sill. Four stories down was the street.

The door from the bath caved in, an axe flashed through it. A policeman thrust arm and shoulder through, a gun in hand.

Wentworth leaped out into space....

CHAPTER 18
A DEAL WITH THE SPIDER

THE COP'S gun spat lead through the window. He twisted the key, thrust open the door and with a rush of others behind him pounded into the room. He raced to the window, peered downward. The sidewalk four stories below was thick with pedestrians, but not one of the moving crowd stared up. There was no morbid circle about a body on the pavement, because there was no body on the pavement!

The cop turned slowly to the room. Commissioner Kirkpatrick was crouched over two bodies on the floor. He straightened, his eye spotted the red seal of the Spider on the wood panel.

He hand stabbed at it. "There!" he spat. "Chop through there. Dougherty, the hall! Cover the next room."

The cop at the window took off his cap and scratched his head. "A guy jumped out here and he ain't on the pavement," he said. "There's no ledge he could walk along, and...."

Kirkpatrick's mouth thinned. "Never mind him," he snapped. "Won't five years of hunting teach you that when the Spider vanishes, he's too fast for any harness bull to catch?"

The cop's mouth fell open. "The Spider!" he cried. "Jeez, is he setting these fires?"

Two men were throwing axes into the secret door. Their edges rang on steel. Dougherty ran back to Kirkpatrick. "Ain't no use hacking that panel," he spluttered. "The next room is empty."

Commissioner Kirkpatrick jerked a hand impatiently. The ax-men halted, rested their tools on the floor and stared after him as he walked slowly to the window.

Kirkpatrick's shoulders were squared angrily. More than twenty men vanished from a room without a trace! Two were dead with the seal of the Spider, and the Spider sprang from a window into thin space. Kirkpatrick's eyes were narrow and bitter. He fingered his wax-pointed mustaches....

Two rooms away from the one which the red council had used, Wentworth climbed into a large trunk.

"You have that list of names, Ram Singh?" he asked his faithful Hindu. Ram Singh was garbed as a porter of the hotel and had a hand-truck ready for the trunk.

"Han Sahib!" The Hindu handed over a folded slip of paper. Wentworth glanced at it, nodded. "Good. Get near that phone again. I'll have further orders for you."

As he spoke, he was winding about his hand a silken cord at the end of which was a padded ring, just large enough for a man's hand to grasp. It was this that had enabled him apparently to jump from the window. Strung from the window of the room 420, which he had taken the previous night, the cord had operated on the principle of a flying ring in a gymnasium. Wentworth had grasped it in one hand and swung off into space. His own weight had swung him, like a pendulum, past the window of the room next door to the council chamber, on the floor below, and to the sill of the room which Ram Singh had taken by himself, posing as a Hindu dignitary.

Wentworth had then climbed in and hauled in the silk cord.

Now he climbed into the specially made trunk with ventilation slits hidden in its sides. Ram Singh locked it shut, put the trunk on the truck and rolled it out into the hall. His posture and movements were precisely those of a porter shuffling along with the truck.

The police made way for him without a second glance.

Wentworth was taken down in the freight elevator in the trunk without interruption. The trunk was placed on a motor truck that bumped away. And presently the hotel was without its surplus porter, Ram Singh.

COMMISSIONER KIRKPATRICK went from the hotel to his usual restaurant, presented his ration card and ate the meager lunch that was allowed by the government, walked out past the manager and the two soldiers who, bayoneted rifles in hand, stood guard over the restaurant. He strode toward the curb, eyes frowning on the walk. A black hat was thrust under his nose and he jerked up his head angrily, stared into the lined old face of an Italian. The man was a hunchback and clasped a violin and a bow beneath his left arm.

"Signor," said the man in a thickly accented voice, "you do not like my playing, yes?"

Kirkpatrick's gray eyes revere impatient as the old man ducked in bows before him. "Yet," continued the old violinist, "I could play a little tune your ears would listen to."

Kirkpatrick turned away with a shrug and signaled a cab. Amusement glinted in the gray-blue eyes of the Italian. A taxi whirred to the curb.

"It would have to be played in private," the old man's voice continued.

Kirkpatrick whirled back and confronted him, gray eyes narrowed suspiciously. "You are hinting at something," he snapped. "Out with it. Who are you?"

The man bowed low over his violin. "Only an old fiddler, sir," he whined, "but I have a tune would please your ear… in private."

"Do you know," snapped Kirkpatrick, "that you are liable to arrest for annoying pedestrians?"

The old man cringed away from his words, put his violin hurriedly in his case. "I am sorry, sir," he mumbled, "I meant no harm, but food prices are so high and a man must live. Some men must live." He inched closer to Kirkpatrick, peered up into his face with quick, bright eyes. "If you will come with me, I will play that tune, and perhaps you will give me food, eh, *signor?*"

Kirkpatrick stood undecided. He was frowning heavily, his gray eyes intent. He was inclined to ignore the man, or to take him to headquarters for questioning, since the fellow kept hinting at knowledge of some sort. But Kirkpatrick had not attained his present position by doing the obvious thing. He was a man who penetrated beneath surfaces. Kirkpatrick abruptly made up his mind. He jerked his head, dismissing the cab.

"Come back into this restaurant," he ordered, "we can find a room here, but I warn you your little tune better be worth hearing."

The violinist chuckled and bobbed his head up and down. "You will enjoy it,   Together, the upright, immaculate police commissioner and the bent old Italian virtuoso went back into the restaurant, and entered a private room on the balcony.

"Now," said Kirkpatrick, "let's hear your tune."

The violinist turned his back to Kirkpatrick and slid onto his finger a ring that was emblazoned with a red spider. He slid a gun from his pocket and, whirling in a crouch, he leveled the pistol at Kirkpatrick with the hand that wore the ring. Kirkpatrick's eyes flashed from gun to ring to the face of the old violinist.

The figure was still crouched, hunch shouldered before him. The head was still twisted up awkwardly with bright, peering eyes, but the face was no longer fawning. The face was grim, with a mouth that was a straight line, the face of Richard Wentworth beneath the disguise of Tito Caliepi.

"I intend you no harm," said a clipped precise voice devoid of all accent, "but it is necessary that you know my identity when I speak—therefore this weapon!"

Kirkpatrick's gray eyes were grim, his mouth tight. He leaned forward on the white-spread table, both hands on its top, and said: "Play your little tune."

Wentworth nodded his head. "Good," he said, "I thought you would be sensible. Those men escaped from the Dorfawl today before you could find them, didn't they?"

Kirkpatrick nodded slowly. "They did. I appreciate you indicating their path, but the panel was of steel, and before we reached the door…" He shrugged one shoulder.

Wentworth touched his breast. "I have here a list of every man who attended that meeting, his name, his address, his position."

KIRKPATRICK'S FACE tightened. He stretched out a hand, palm upward. His eyes glinted. Wentworth shook his head slowly. "Not yet. I have a proposal to make."

"If it's a pardon," Kirkpatrick said quickly, "I'll string the governor up by his thumbs if necessary to get it."

A wintry smile twisted Wentworth's lips. "Since when has the Spider asked things for himself, Mr. Commissioner?" he asked. "No, it is something infinitely more necessary but more dangerous to yourself."

"Name it!" Kirkpatrick bit out the words.

Wentworth eyed him directly, blue-gray eyes meeting eyes of gray. "You do not ask for proof that this list of names is authentic, or ask whether I can prove them guilty?" he asked softly.

Kirkpatrick's lips lifted slightly, twitching the black militant points of his mustache. "If you, the Spider, say it is accurate, I do not question it. If the men are guilty"—his face hardened; his jaw jutted strongly—"I do not need proof. I'll get it from them."

Wentworth nodded briefly. "Thank you," he said. "My proposal is this: Tonight the Food Destroyers strike again. They are planning a decoy fire to draw protection from their real goal. I do not know their real goal. I want ten of your radio cars, manned by men who will unquestioningly obey my orders."

Kirkpatrick straightened slowly, brows drawn tightly together, lids eyes staring into Wentworth's. "It would cost my job," he said, as if to himself.

Wentworth nodded slowly. "But it may smash the gang for all time," he said. "There is one thing more I want to tell you. One of the men in the room is not listed here. He hid his face while passing through the halls so that the man who spied could not see it. Even if you seize every man on the list, that one, with the gangs, will be powerful enough to carry on. In fact, if he could, that man would be pleased to kill every other member of the syndicate, so that he himself could reap the profits."

Kirkpatrick frowned. "This is your reason for wanting the police cars?"

"Yes," said Wentworth briefly. "I want to wipe out the gangs that are this man's tools, then I will go to him for the reckoning."

"You know him?"

Wentworth shook his head slowly. "I think I know him. I will know how to reach him when the time comes." His face was completely serious. The red Spider seal glowed on his hand.

Abruptly there was a terrific crashing clatter of glass breaking, shouts and yells. The sounds came from below stairs.

Kirkpatrick darted to the door, yanked it open, peered down from the balcony. A band of thirty men, starved, gaunt wretches with haggard faces, had crashed the windows, were charging the food counters.

THE MANAGER, pistol in hand, the two soldiers with leveled rifles beside him, stood on the counter.

"Men," he pleaded, "don't force me to shoot. Believe me, I sympathize with you from the bottom of my heart. I cannot give you food without your ration tickets, even if you could pay for it."

A howl went up from the men. A wild-haired, unshaven man sprang to the front ranks, whirled and faced the mob. "He can't kill more than four or five of us. The rest of us can eat. And the dead can't starve to death."

He whirled toward the manager. "Give up your gun."

Wentworth squeezed past Kirkpatrick, sprang to the railing of the balcony.

"Just a minute, men," he called. It was a commanding voice. Every face in the restaurant stared upward at him. Gone was the hunch from his shoulders, gone the crouching servility of the old violinist. He stood stalwart and strong.

"Men," he said, "I promise you that tonight the gang that has been destroying food will be wiped out. The government is rushing fresh supplies here. They will not be destroyed. I do not promise that you will have plenty to eat tomorrow, or next week. But I do promise that the destruction of food will cease and that relief will begin at once."

The wild-haired man spun toward him, shook a fist. "Yeh!" he shouted. "Who are you that you can promise things like that?"

Wentworth smiled. His lips bared on tusklike teeth that glinted savagely. His shoulders distorted, and an evil face leered down from the balcony. He laid his hand on the rail and the seal of the Spider glowed.

Dead silence fell on the crowd below.

"I am the Spider," he said sibilantly. "Tonight I kill the destroyers of food!" He turned and darted into the room whence he had come.

He faced Kirkpatrick across the table. The Commissioner's face was tense. No gun was in Wentworth's hand now. He held a folded piece of paper. He smiled slowly, reached up his hand and removed the celluloid tusks which masked his teeth.

"Quick, Kirkpatrick, what is your decision? My friends, the police, will be here in a moment, looking for the Spider, and I must be gone."

Kirkpatrick stretched out his hand, not for the paper, but for the hand of the Spider.

"It's a deal," he said simply.

Wentworth clasped his hand for a moment, laid the paper on the table and caught up his violin. He crossed to the window, peered out. A moment sufficed to string his double silken cord, to twist it about his leg.

"You'll find most of those men at Glastonbury's meeting at the Dorfawl," he said. "I'll phone later for details." He slid down the cord to the alley that passed behind the restaurant.

When police stampeded minutes later into the room with drawn guns, Kirkpatrick was sipping coffee there. A slip of paper lay on the table before him, a slip of paper containing nineteen names.

CHAPTER 19
THE SPIDER STRIKES

WENTWORTH SPENT the afternoon in rapid preparation. He phoned Professor Brownlee that he needed a short wave radio that would operate from an automobile. He phoned Kirkpatrick and got a list of the numbers of the cars assigned to him. These cars were to obey only signals signed with the symbol, S4.

"I've got those nineteen men whom you listed locked in cells," Kirkpatrick told him. "Though it's apt to cost me my job if I can't make them talk."

"They'll talk after tonight," Wentworth promised him grimly.

"Have you seen the papers?" Kirkpatrick asked. "They've got

your balcony scene complete, including a detailed description of yourself."

"Thanks," said Wentworth softly.

He asked if the radio cars could be equipped with Thompson sub-machine guns, firing incendiary bullets and Kirkpatrick, after a conference with army officials, arranged it.

Then Wentworth disguised more youthfully than old Tito went to the Women's Detention House where Nita was a prisoner. He took a stand upon the platform of the elevated railway structure which had a station at the corner, and sere-naded her with his violin. And Wentworth began and closed his serenade with "Whispering Hope."

It had been over a month since Wentworth had learned Nita was a prisoner. For three weeks of that time he had been vir-tually in a coma from his wound. During the past week, he had communicated with her through a lawyer, but all his efforts to release her had proved in vain. Glastonbury and the courts incensed by the depredations of the Destroyers, combined to keep behind bars anyone suspected of connivance, as Gaston-bury insisted she was. Wentworth had rained luxuries upon her anonymously, to the enragement of Glastonbury, who sought frantically to trace the gifts to their source, knowing that they must come from Wentworth.

It was not a joyful serenade that Wentworth delivered. Through it ran threads of melancholy, too. For tonight, he well knew that he battled with the forces of half the underworlds of the entire earth.

The Spider had planned well, but the Spider was only mortal.

As the last car roared past with blazing guns, he slammed one of the
bombs against the windshield, another in the path of the tires.

As a prelude to the bitter battle he planned to resume the disguise of Tito Caliepi. In that role, he knew, the gunmen of the Destroyers searched for him. They would seek to remove the man who promised to thwart all their plans.

Since the newspapers had broadcast that description, Wentworth knew he had only to show himself on the sidewalks to be spotted. Tito's had been a deliberately conspicuous figure—a hunchback with a black cape. Yes, surely such a man would be spotted anywhere.

Wentworth drove doleful thoughts from his mind, and put joy into his playing. Dusk was coming now and with it the breath of a chill wind. Wentworth, to the singing strains of "Whispering Hope" concluded for the applauding audience on the platform and returned to his rooms as night fell.

That move was at once safer, yet more dangerous. Fewer would see, but those that saw, if they were the guns of the gangs, would be better able to kill. And it was Wentworth's intention that the killers should meet him!

Where would the killers look for him? They would have intelligent direction, that much was certain, for the master of the Destroyers had not been taken in with the others of the red council.

FIRST OF all then, the killers would look for him about the hide-outs of the Destroyers themselves. Where these were located, Wentworth did not know, except that Janice Hally had called an unlisted phone he couldn't trace in the Sky building. Second, they would look for him at spots where he might locate their fires, around airports.

But the wind was mounting; clouds were piling up. A storm was brewing and planes could not take the air for long. If they did, their visibility would soon be cut to the point that they would be useless. High buildings, then, remained.

Wentworth smiled to himself, the twisted toothy smile of Tito Caliepi. The Sky building would be first choice. Two reasons then for going there. Down grade on Fifth Avenue toward the Sky building, Wentworth walked slowly with the sweep of the wind behind him. Behind him, a few blocks up the Avenue, this mad chase had begun, up there where a fire bomb had been tossed into the limousine of Hanford Tyson. And he was coming here to end it, coming here to be a target for fire bombs, for the Destroyers' bullets.

He hobbled, a twisted, hunchbacked figure driven by the wind into the grand entrance of the Sky building, on into the gaudy rotunda. The big wind gauge fluctuated with the changing velocity of the wind that swept a fifth of a mile upward where the building of man scraped the sky.

He entered the tower elevator with four others who paid their dollars to view the city from the clouds, a man and a girl wedged in a corner together, fingers interlaced; a woman with a small boy stood near him. The car sighed upward and deposited them in a gallery of windows.

Wentworth hobbled on down the corridor to the car that would carry him still higher to the open balcony with its breast-high rampart where the wind was cold and free. There the city would be laid out below, in spangled patterns of light and shadow. There the guns might wait for the Spider.

169

Wentworth made a slow circuit of the balcony, scanning the people who gazed out over the city. Not a suspicious figure in the lot. A thin smile played across his mouth. Perhaps he was early for his rendezvous with death. He peered out over the city and, suddenly as he stared, a red spike of fire thrust up from the western horizon!

Wentworth's eyes narrowed. Obviously the decoy fire. It would have to be started first. Excited cries nearby told that others had spotted the mounting horror of the night.

"It's those bombs again!" a man's voice exclaimed. "Damn those profiteers!"

Wentworth remained motionless by the railing. Other towers of flame joined the first until they did a sawtooth dance along the West side, throwing out long streamers in the shouting wind.

Wentworth figured the fire had started on West Sixteenth Street, near the freight terminal. Below, the street shrilled with the sirens of the fire equipment. Company after company raced past, swept on to the scene. Wentworth clenched a fist at his side. Damn it! They were stripping the city of equipment. There would be none left when the real blow was struck.

Wentworth whirled and strode back to the elevator. He raced to a telephone booth, excitedly rang up Kirkpatrick.

"For heaven's sake, man," he cried, "don't let them send all the equipment to that West side fire. That's only the decoy—the real blow comes later."

Kirkpatrick's voice over the phone was grim. "The mayor has taken over the police department. I'm just a supernumerary. So far he hasn't found out about those cars for you, but I'm expecting any minute...."

A shadow on the glass jerked Wentworth's head toward the door. Then he dropped the receiver and slumped to the bottom of the booth, a gun spitting in his hand.

The man standing outside the booth swayed. The machine gun in his hand barked in brief thunder, bullets spattering the glass, boring through the booth. Wentworth fired twice more into the head of the machine gunner. The head fell back. The man slapped to the floor.

Wentworth jerked erect, snapped open the door and dived to the floor beside the machine gunner. From a darkened doorway a pistol racketed, streaming lead at him. WENTWORTH FIRED carefully at the flash, heard a man curse. Police whistles were shrilling. Building guards were slapping flat feet to the paved floor in frantic haste. A shadow detached itself from the darkened doorway and fled for the exit. Wentworth, gun ready in his hand, shuffled after him.

He dodged out of the door. The wounded man was skulking through shadows across the street. For a moment his face was painted white by the headlights of a fire truck gorging around the corner and Wentworth recognized him. The wounded man was the dope addict who had dogged his trail since the beginning of this crusade against crime. More equipment went racing to the West side fire. Wentworth cursed. The mayor was crippling the city.

Wentworth ducked across the street, followed the fleeing gunman. He grabbed a taxi when the gunman did and swept eastward, then north. The cab ahead stopped and Wentworth's quarry reeled from it. The taxi was gone at once. Wentworth spilled out of his machine, gave the driver half a torn twenty dollar bill.

"You get the rest when I come back," he snapped. "Get around the corner and wait."

The staggering figure ahead moved slowly into a dark doorway, thrust his way upstairs. Wentworth pushed in after him, eased upward in deathly darkness. He heard voices raised in excitement.

"You damned fool! Why did you come here?" the reprimand was shrill.

The whining voice of the dope addict replied. "How in hell could I go in anywhere and phone with blood dripping off'n me?"

Wentworth crept closer to the door.

"Who's going to fix my arm?" the man whined. "I had to tell you the Spider called the police and told them to lay off the West side fire. I had to do that, didn't I? Say, who's going to fix my arm?"

"I'll fix it," the first man snarled. A pistol cracked twice.

Coarse laughter rang. "You fixed it all right."

"Come on, let's go," the snarler said. "Toss that out in the street with a fire bomb to hug."

Wentworth ducked back down the stairs, swung around the corner to his cab. "How much for the taxi?" he demanded.

The driver stored at him, narrow-eyed. "What's the big idea?"

"I'm going places you won't want to go," Wentworth told him shortly. "So I'll drive. Here's a thousand."

The driver stared at the bills. Wentworth took the man's cap while he counted money, jostled him up the street. "Get the hell away from here."

"Sure," said the driver joyfully. "When you get through with the car, dump it in the river."

Wentworth, the cape tossed into the back of the cab with his black hat, dragged on the taxi driver's cap and sent the taxi humming around the corner. He was just in time to pick up the trail of the four men who had grabbed a speedy car from a nearby garage. They sped uptown.

The eyes of the Spider gleamed joyously. When the hood who had tried to rub him out had reported him as having told the police the first fire was a decoy, these men had decided to get under way. The inference was that they were involved in the second fire. The car ahead was skimming at forty up the East side. Wentworth trailed.

Ten blocks of that and another powerful auto swung into the wake of the first. Two blocks more and another joined the parade. The gangs were rallying! Wentworth jerked his head about to peer behind.

A black limousine was charging toward him. Street lights glinted on gun muzzles. Wentworth wrenched the wheel crazily and machine-gun bullets ripped through the cab.

Wentworth threw himself to the floorboards clutched the wheel with one hand and guided the cab, swerving wildly, straight for the show window of a store closed for the night. More bullets clanged into the car. The front wheels cracked the curb, bounced high and the taxi took a nose dive through the window.

The windshield slammed back and broke in fragments over Wentworth's back. He peered out cautiously, gun ready. The cars had raced on. He wriggled clear. His flashlight spotted a phone. He called Ram Singh, got an instant answer.

"Tell all cars waiting for S4 signals to converge on upper Second Avenue, north of Sixtieth Street," he snapped. "They'll find a chain of cars, traveling fast. They're gang cars. Open fire with incendiary bullets. Pick me up at Third and Forty-Second."

Wentworth darted out of the store, snatching cape and hat from the cab, and raced for the corner where he had ordered Ram Singh to meet him. The Hindu would call the orders he had directed over the portable radio set in the auto, pick him up with that car and permit Wentworth to direct the chase.

Scarcely had Wentworth reached the corner, when Ram Singh whirled a Chevrolet sedan out of Third Avenue and picked him up.

"Second Avenue," Wentworth ordered swiftly. "North."

The Chevrolet crashed through traffic lights, swept northward. The chain of gang cars had swept from sight. "Faster!" Wentworth barked.

The speedometer needled up to sixty, wavered higher. Wentworth picked up the radio transmitter, spotted a street sign at Sixty-Seventh.

"S4 now at Second Avenue and Sixty Seventh Street. Haven't sighted gang cars. S4."

The Chevrolet swept on. Wentworth leaned forward, studying the scanty traffic ahead. Then he saw two cars shoot west from the Avenue.

"West," Wentworth snapped. The Chevrolet took the corner on two wheels, skated fenders with a Lincoln and darted on with blaring horn. They crashed a light at Third, slammed into Park swaying wildly, shot north.

"S4 calling," Wentworth barked into the transmitter. "Watch all transverse park roads. Cars heading west."

TEN BLOCKS ahead up Park Avenue, Wentworth spotted a black car he knew. It was the limousine from which he had been gunned out of the taxi.

"S4 calling. Gang cars now at Eighty-Second and Park Avenue. "Watch Eighty-Sixth Street transverse through park, Ninety-Seventh Street, transverse. Open fire with incendiary bullets on sight. Cars carrying fire bombs. S4."

The cars ahead sped on past Eighty-Sixth and now the Chevrolet was crowding close at their heels. A police car ripped past him with siren going full tilt.

"Cut that siren. S4," he barked into the transmitter.

The siren choked, but it was too late. A machine-gun cackled from the black limousine. The police car ground-looped into the grass strip that split Park Avenue, dived across the south-bound lane of traffic and wrapped around an electric light post.

The entire line of gang cars swung west then and Wentworth counted as they streamed across Park Avenue to the left. There were seventeen of them. All heavy, powerful cars, all sedans, probably equipped with bullet-proof glass.

"S4 calling. Seventeen gang cars turning west off Park Avenue into Ninety-Third. They just machine-gunned two police who used their siren. Open fire on sight. S4."

Wentworth sent Ram Singh whirling the wrong way on east-bound Ninety-Second street, spun out into Fifth Avenue even with the first of the gang cars. A burst of machine-gun fire heralded nine police cars in echelon. The leading gang car swirled northward into Fifth Avenue, plowed through the nine-fold stream of machine gun fire. Its tires exploded but its windows held firm. Its own machine-guns bellowed an answer.

Cars swinging out into Fifth behind it threw their own batteries into the battle.

The first gang car roared on, swaying wildly with punctured tires. Machine-guns flickered and coughed from its windows. A police car swerved to meet it like a frightened horse, its driver leaning back, dead at the wheel. It rammed the sedan nose on. The Ford bounced back, skittered sideways into the curb, toppled and rolled over twice, then landing, it bounced on its tires.

The sedan swung wildly left, rammed a second police Ford, and raced on to meet the stone wall of Central Park. It struck at an angle, twisted and slammed sideways into it. Its rear swung out, caught a tree and stopped. The front kept going, made a half circuit and its front axle dropped over the gutter.

Flames belched out within it in an explosion that hurled bullet-proof glass fifty feet. A score of incendiary bombs had let go in the same instant. The men did not even scream.

The other gang cars raced on. Two police cars whirled and followed. The rest were wrecked, or their officers killed. Wentworth ordered Ram Singh to enter Central Park at Ninety-Sixth. The Chevrolet raced northward at top speed.

"Delay those gang cars at all costs. S4," Wentworth barked into the mike.

Almost at once, machine guns were ripping loose again. Those two lone police cars had overtaken the gangsters and were giving battle.

Ram Singh sent the auto wheeling out 110th Street traffic "East!" barked Wentworth. East they raced. A double-deck green bus was lumbering along, almost empty. "Stall that bus!"

Ram Singh jammed it to the curb. Wentworth was out instantly, a gun in each hand. In one minute he had cleared the bus of the driver and three passengers. With a gesture to Ram Singh, he sprang to the driver's seat. Ram Singh climbed aboard laboriously, carrying a sheet of steel with a glass peephole near its top.

Instantly, Wentworth slammed the bus into motion. He clamped his hand on the horn and held it there, forcing the bus to thirty-five. Traffic jumped the curb to escape.

WENTWORTH WHIRLED into Fifth Avenue. The gang cars were three blocks south, just getting under way again. Wentworth jammed the accelerator to the floor. Ram Singh supported the bullet-proof shield before him, crouched behind it himself. Wildly the bus careened, gathering more momentum.

Before the first gang car could get going fast, Wentworth charged into it. It was not a direct hit, but a side-scraping blow that slammed the car against the curbing and sheered its wheels off. Its body crushed in as if it were tin.

Wentworth charged on for the next car. Behind him flames leaped out wildly. The second car whirled to escape and Wentworth rammed the blunt nose of the bus into its rear as it turned around, sent it sailing in a slow end-over-end whirl, fifty feet down the street. There it draped itself over the hood of a third gang car. The blast of flames rose twenty feet high.

Neither collision had more than slowed the heavy bus. Wentworth jockeyed the bus, jammed the accelerator down. Frantically gangster cars were trying to flee from his path. Backing and racing motors, two of them collided and were enveloped in flames. The black limousine with stuttering machine guns raced straight toward Wentworth.

Bullets hammered the windshield into fragments. A geyser of steam answered the lead that plowed through the radiator. Another gang car near the right-hand curb, trapped between the pyres of two comrades, started a wild left-hand swing to escape the bus. Wentworth swerved to the left, put a snapped pistol bullet through a tire.

The car yawed out of control, slammed its side into the nose of the black limousine and spilled liquid flame over it. The black car pivoted on its nose and Wentworth's bus rammed the rear as it came around.

The car's wheels were still churning at top speed. Its nose pointing back the way it had come, it raced with a dead man at the wheel, twisting, wrenching at furious pace, back into the line of the gangsters. Three more cars went up in smoke.

Wentworth yanked the wheel, cleared the flaming mess and plowed down upon the rest. The bus was a wreck now. Its radiator, battered back against the engine, was spewing steam. The front wheels wobbled crazily. Not a window remained in the entire vehicle. But the engine still rattled valiantly.

Wentworth accurately took the left front wheel off an entire role of gang cars, pot-shooting with his automatics. The gangsters, terrified, spewed from the flaming cars.

Only one machine remained now. It was trapped by the hulk of the black car, strewn with another auto across the street, between that and the bus. Wentworth wrenched the wheel to send the bus charging this last foe—and the left front wheel of the bus wrenched loose.

The gangster car spurted toward Wentworth, machine-gun yammering. Wentworth sprang from a side window. He wrenched open the door of an abandoned gangster car which had not burst into flames. In the tonneau rested a steel box. A jerk, and its top was off revealing gleaming rows of glass cylinders.

Wentworth snatched three, sprang to the cover of the bus. As the gang car roared past with blazing guns, he slammed one of the bombs against the windshield, another in the path of the tires.

Two bursts of flame. The driver, blinded, tried to hold a true course. Fire ate at his tires, fire ran in a stream down over the hood, dripped in on the engine. Fire, blown by the wind, thrust inquisitive fingers in ventilators.

Screams tore from within the car. A door fanned open, slammed back against the body of the car. Wentworth threw another bomb, and saw the gangster car careen with a final splintering crash into the wrecks of others.

The Spider straightened from his crouch behind the bus, stared about him at the carnage he had wrought. He saw what was left of the gangsters who had paid for their wholesale killings, for the sufferings of starving thousands, for the impoverishment of a nation. He looked about him and laughed a little wildly, then took out a cigarette lighter from his pocket.

While Ram Singh stared at him fixedly, Wentworth walked to the nose of the bus and imprinted the red seal with its hairy, gruesome legs upon the scarred, tarnished brass of the bus' radiator.

"A decoration of honor this time," Wentworth told Ram Singh. Then the sardonic humor went from his face and an ugly light glinted deep in his eyes.

"We have balked the Destroyers, killed many of them, but one remains, Ram Singh," he said softly. "And that one is the greatest fiend of them all. Where is the home of Janice Hally?"

CHAPTER 20
CONDEMNED TO THE FIRE

RAM SINGH'S dark eyes glinted. With Wentworth striding behind, he hurried eastward until they found a taxi. The cab spun southward, took them to East Sixty-Sixth Street.

"The apartment number is 10 G," said Ram Singh.

Wentworth nodded. "Good work! Usual orders from now on."

He strode into the apartment house, took an automatic elevator to the tenth floor. When he left the cab, he was again the hunchbacked old violinist. Tito Caliepi was the Spider.

He rang the bell of 10 G. A peephole ticked aside and a girl's eye stared out at him. Wentworth saw the eye narrow, saw it search the hall behind and around him. The door jerked open.

"Come in," said Janice Hally.

Wentworth nodded amiably and shambled in. Nor did he wince when the door slammed shut and a gun jabbed into his ribs.

"Come on, boys," the girl sang out. "I've got the Spider!"

"Aw, quit fooling and come on back," a man called.

"I'm coming," the girl laughed sharply. "But I'm coming with the Spider." She jabbed Wentworth's back again. "Get going, boy friend."

Wentworth chuckled, ambled on into a room where two men lounged at ease on a davenport. At sight of him, they snapped to their feet; two men, one bulky, but alert on his feet as a boxer, the other short and with a face as sharp as a cheese knife.

Shorty pulled his mouth together first. "Well, well, Janice, how'd you come by this?" he jeered.

"It just rang the bell and walked in," said the girl.

"Hell," exclaimed Shorty. He snaked a gun from his hip and stalked the hall.

"There's nobody down there," Janice called.

The heavier man came toward Wentworth on his toes. His

head seemed to hunch further down between his shoulders. "So you're the guy who got us canned from the police force!"

Wentworth raised his brows and smiled thinly. "I didn't know it, but it's good news," he said. "From the minute you let those fake cops into Xavier Jones' apartment, you were labeled crooked."

"Yeah!" The man's right fist shot out, but the Spider continued to smile and the blow fanned air as he pulled his head aside.

"Don't do that again," he said gently.

The detective ducked his bull head and waded in with both fists swinging. Wentworth swayed out of his path, shot his left in below the man's ear. The man tumbled to the floor and lay on his belly, breathing hoarsely.

Without warning, a blow smashed against the back of Wentworth's head and he stumbled to his knees. His hat and wig saved him most of the injury but he was half-stunned. He twisted his head, peered up into the dead-white face of the girl. Her eyes were like blue flame.

"Don't think you can get away," she said harshly.

Shorty came back in the room, paused with his gun leveled. "What the hell is this?"

The girl told him. Shorty made a soft whistling between his lips.

"Like that, eh?" He crossed behind Wentworth and ground the barrel of his revolver into the back of his neck. It hurt. Wentworth crumpled forward on the floor.

"**LAY OFF** him," the girl ordered, gesturing with her gun.

"What the hell?" Shorty sounded surprised. "You crack him and I just want to enjoy a little clean fun, too, and—"

"Lay off him!" bit out the girl.

"All right, all right," Shorty agreed hastily.

"All right," the girl echoed. "Now call the chief and tell him we got this babe here and see what he wants."

"Sa-ay," Shorty had turned admiring now. "There's wisdom in them words."

Wentworth heard a phone dial zipping, heard the boxer groan, start to his feet.

"Chief?" came Shorty's voice. "Listen, we got the Spider here. No. He's a prisoner. The gal took him... just walked in and she jabbed a gun in his ribs... No. There ain't nobody else around. Okay, Chief, in five minutes."

The phone clattered. "Chief says bring him to the Empire State offices."

In the taxi, the wind revived Wentworth completely but his head still ached from the girl's blow. They went into the Empire State building in a close knot, took an elevator to a floor in the thirties. Here they shoved Wentworth ahead into an office without names on its ground glass panels. Behind an elaborate desk sat a man in tuxedo, his head hidden in a hood of red velvet.

He had his hands on top the desk, toying with a cylinder of glass which contained a greenish liquid. A fire bomb.

"This is an unexpected pleasure," the voice came softly, muffled by the mask. "I can't be too emphatic about both angles of that statement, but I want especially to stress the pleasure."

He stood up, dangling keys on his fingers. "You three have done well," he said. "You will be well repaid. You can go now."

"Perhaps you don't know, Shorty," Wentworth said softly, "that you are the only members of his gang that aren't either dead or in prison."

The chief took a quick step forward and struck Wentworth heavily on the mouth. The Spider's smile remained.

"That is confirmation of the truth," said the Spider.

Shorty looked at his bulky partner, winked slowly. "I guess we'll just stick around," he said, "and collect."

"Fools," spat out the chief. "What do you expect to profit by defying me?"

Shorty spun his revolver on his forefinger. "Well, I'll tell you, Chief," he said. "If we turn this bozo over to headquarters, we'll collect around twenty-five grand each in rewards."

Wentworth held his peace. He had started the conflict, but now he kept out of it. His guns had been removed from him before they had started for the office of the chief. He was without any weapon… except his brain. But he had deliberately walked into Janice Hally's power because he knew she would take him to the chief. When this man was eliminated, the gang would be wiped out completely.

"Drop that gun, Shorty," the girl said huskily.

She spoke from behind him and nudged him with the pistol barrel. With a curse, he complied. The chief snatched out a revolver and covered Wentworth and the other man.

"Nice work, Janice," he said, "take the big one's gun, too."

The girl did.

"Now listen to me," the chief spat out. "You two can hang

around, and my promise still stands. But don't get it into your heads you can run things."

Shorty hitched up his trousers. "Not while the girl's around, we can't," he said gloomily.

A smile still lingered about Wentworth's mouth. It showed the inch-long tusks of celluloid. Two of the gang's members were unarmed, now. It would be easier to handle two guns than four.

The chief turned toward Wentworth. "You keep those two covered while I take care of Mr. Spider," he said softly to the girl, and he leveled his pistol at Wentworth. "Where would you rather be shot first?" he asked gently.

"No!" said Janice sharply.

The chief's head swung sharply toward her, but there was irritation in the movement. "Now what's the matter?"

"He must die by fire," the girl said in a harsh monotone, "the same as Denny did. They promised me that."

"By fire!" agreed the chief.

HIS EYES dropped for a second to the glass bomb on his desk, with its oily green liquid of flame. He looked up again and his eyes glowed. "How does that strike you, Spider?"

Wentworth's face contorted. He shrank back across the room until his back brought up against the wall.

"Ah! It doesn't appeal to you, eh?" asked the chief. "That's fine." He straightened, the gun still competently held. He thrust the fire bomb into his pocket. "We'll go to the tower," he announced. "Put Shorty's cuffs on the Spider, Janice."

Wentworth's face still was terror-stricken. He seemed

185

bemused with fear as the girl snapped the handcuffs on his wrists under cover of the chief's gun.

"You know that was really an excellent idea of yours, Janice," the hooded man said gloatingly. "The Spider will burn where all the city can see. Tomorrow they will know that the Destroyers still rule. With him out of the way, I can build a new gang...."

Janice stepped back, gun in hand. "Now you two boys take charge of the Spider and see that he behaves himself," the chief ordered. "And see that you behave yourselves, too. Remember, we have the guns."

The two men roughed Wentworth out of the office, down a corridor to an elevator that stood with the door open, an operator waiting. He glanced incuriously at Wentworth, touched his cap to the red-hooded chief and the car shot upward.

At the top of the shaft, the operator went with them to the cage that went to the base of the mooring mast, but even then the chief was not satisfied.

"You wait here," he instructed the three of them. "See that no one comes outside."

The two men looked at each other in a silence through which the mournful whine of the wind raised its voice.

"Okay," said Shorty, "we wait here."

Wentworth smiled at the girl. Her mouth compressed. She thrust forward. "I'm going along," she said stubbornly.

"Pleasant person, aren't you?" grunted the chief. "All right, come along."

He thrust Wentworth out first, followed with a leveled gun, the girl at his elbow. The wind swooped down on them. It whipped off Wentworth's hat, sent it sailing into black space, jerked at his lank hair.

The chief threw back his red-masked head and laughed. There was wildness in his voice.

"Higher! Higher!" he shouted. "Who can see the Destroyers' light behind a five-foot rampart?"

He thrust Wentworth violently toward the open iron-work stairway that led upward to the balcony of the mooring mast far above.

Wentworth checked his rush with his shoulder against the iron railing, whirled to face the chief and the girl. Her head was bare and the wind tugged at her streaming red hair, pulled it loose and flaunted it like a flag of fire.

"You fool," Wentworth hurled out. "Do you think you can get away with murdering the Spider. Do you think that I have not left record of your identity?"

"Get up the stairs," the chief ordered. His leveled pistol glinted in the light from the open doorway.

Wentworth slowly moved backward up the steps, the other following. He threw back his head and laughed. "You and that red-headed fool of a girl, who thinks I killed her Denny. Do you remember," he demanded of her, "what day you last saw your Denny?"

"Yes, I remember," the girl said tightly, "as if I could forget anything about Denny!"

"Shut up," snapped the chief. "Get up those stairs."

"You see," Wentworth threw at the girl. "He's trying to keep me from talking because—"

"Get up those stairs!" It was a shout of rage.

Wentworth had checked his ascent. Before the threat of that lifted gun, he retreated one more step. "You won't shoot me," he told the chief calmly. "You're too anxious to burn me... *like you did Denny!*"

THE GUN in the chief's hand spat crimson. A sledge hammer struck Wentworth's left shoulder, slammed him back upon the steps. He thrust himself up. His voice rose triumphantly.

"You see, Janice," he cried. "He doesn't want me to talk about Denny."

"I don't give a damn how much you talk," the chief howled. "Get up those stairs."

The chief stood near the bottom of the stairs, his red-hooded head thrust forward, the girl just behind him. The moon peeped a frightened white face from behind the clouds and its light fell on the girl's face. She was frowning.

"Wait a minute," she said shortly. "I want this boy to burn, not die with a bullet. That's too easy."

Wentworth fought off the dizziness of pain, the weakness of the wound. He raised his heavy head.

"What day did your Denny disappear, Janice?" he shouted.

"Give me that gun," snapped the girl. "I told you I want him to die by fire, not bullets."

With her own weapon threatening, she took the gun from the chief's hand. The chief climbed two steps so that he was not more than ten feet from Wentworth. He took the gleaming cylinder of liquid fire from his pocket, hefted it in his hand.

The girl moved in front of him, a gun in each hand. Her red hair streamed across her face like storm clouds across the moon.

"Denny disappeared on March 12th," she said.

"March 12th," said Wentworth "the same day that Hanford Tyson is *supposed* to have died."

"What do you mean?" it was a cry.

"I mean," Wentworth said sharply, spilling his words out rapidly, "that the man with that red hood on, the head of the Destroyers, is Hanford Tyson. He burned your Denny in his automobile to make everyone believe he was dead…."

An inarticulate cry tore from the hooded man. "It's a lie!"

"I had Kirkpatrick exhume the body they called Tyson," Wentworth rushed on, "and his teeth were not Tyson's teeth. That is Hanford Tyson behind you. *Take off his mask!*"

The girl whirled toward Tyson, snatched at the red velvet hood. Her gun struck the man's head and half stunned him. He clung to the railing with one hand and she snatched the hood from his head. The pale, heavy-jowled face of Hanford Tyson stared at her!

"You killed my Denny," the girl cried. "You're going to burn for it!"

She snatched for the glass bomb in the man's hand. He held it upward at arm's length. The girl struck him in the face with her gun, snatched for it with her other hand.

"Look out, for God's sake!" Tyson screamed.

The gun in the girl's hand struck the glass knob and the thick, greenish liquid spilled down over them, spilled down over

Janice's red hair, over her body, down upon the gray head of Hanford Tyson.

Only for an instant was it a liquid, then it burst into dazzling flame. Tyson screamed. The girl's red hair became living red flame.

The two figures struggled and writhed, wrapped in flame. They reeled against the iron railing, toppled and were gone! They pitched off into space, spun and tumbled downward like a ball from a Roman candle, like a blazing comet, their screams rising to the heavens, then dwindling, melting into the wild keening of the wind.

Wentworth reeled drunkenly to his feet, crazy laughter in his throat. He snatched up a gun the girl had dropped and staggered toward the tower. The figure of Ram Singh, turbaned, graceful, stood full in the doorway and bowed, cupped hands to his forehead.

Wentworth reeled into the hallway, stared at two bodies huddled against the wall, two bodies of men, one short and one tall, with knife wounds in their breasts.

"They forbade me to come to your assistance, *Sahib*," said Ram Singh. "When I had settled the controversy, there was no need of my assistance."

Wentworth dropped the gun. It clanked on the floor. "So you followed... orders, as usual... Ram Singh?"

The Spider's knees buckled and he slid to the floor.

CHAPTER 21
A MATTER OF EVIDENCE

WENTWORTH'S LEFT arm was in a black sling. Nita Van Sloan was at his right and there was a smile on her lips that would not come off.

Wentworth was being arraigned for murder.

District Attorney Glastonbury strode up and down before the Judge's bench, his short little legs fairly bouncing him around. "This is the most ridiculous, the most outrageous thing I ever heard of," he declared vociferously, "calling witnesses at a preliminary hearing!"

He pivoted, thrust out an arm like a ramrod at Wentworth. "This is once," he shouted, "when all your trickery won't get you off!"

Wentworth smiled at him cheerfully, turned to Nita and made a remark behind his hand. She threw back her head and laughed softly. "Dick," she said, "you're simply impossible."

The judge was leaning forward over the bench. He was ruddy, and the white hair was like a drift of snow above his forehead.

"I see nothing irregular about the proceedings, Mr. District Attorney," he said gravely. "The prisoner has refused to waive preliminary examination, which means you must show you have a case against him. You've presented a few witnesses. He has every right to call his." He slapped his gavel on the bench. "Call the first witness for the defense."

The clerk stood and monotoned: "John Glastonbury. John Glastonbury."

Glastonbury glared at Wentworth, then crossed to the stand and was sworn. Wentworth, who was acting as his own attorney, rose and, clearing his throat, stalked across to Glastonbury's side.

"What date, Mr. Glastonbury," he asked, does your affidavit specify that Hanford Tyson died?"

"March 12th," Glastonbury bit off the words.

"On what date was Tyson buried?"

"March 13th."

"That is all," said Wentworth, turning back to his seat. "State may cross-examine."

Glastonbury stepped down from the stand, cheeks puffed out angrily.

The judge leaned forward, peering beneath raised brows. "Does the State wish to cross-examine?"

"No!" shouted Glastonbury, then added, more meekly, "Your Honor."

"Call the next witness."

"Stanley Kirkpatrick! Stanley Kirkpatrick!"

The police commissioner, trim as ever, smiling beneath the neat points of his mustache, took the stand. Wentworth crossed to his side gravely.

"Mr. Kirkpatrick, did you issue an exhumation permit for the body of Hanford Tyson, died March 12th, buried March 13th?"

"I obtained an exhumation permit and personally supervised the opening of the grave," he said slowly.

"What?" Glastonbury was on his feet.

Wentworth turned coldly toward him. "You may cross-examine presently, Mr. District Attorney." He turned back to Kirkpatrick. "What did you do with the body, Mr. Kirkpatrick?"

"I permitted an examination of the teeth by Dr. Jimpson Hughes."

WENTWORTH WALKED away, waving his hand toward Glastonbury. The attorney was up like a spring, bouncing to the side of Kirkpatrick's chair. He stabbed a bony finger into Kirkpatrick's face.

"Who signed that exhumation order?" he demanded.

Kirkpatrick raised his brows, "You did."

"I!" Glastonbury was spluttering with rage. "I...."

Kirkpatrick drew a folded paper from his pocket. "It may have escaped your attention in the press of business, but here it is."

"May I see that?" inquired the Judge.

Kirkpatrick passed it over. "Quite in order," commented the Judge, "and signed by yourself. Are there any further questions?"

"No," said Glastonbury, "Your Honor."

Kirkpatrick stepped down. The clerk intoned, "Dr. Jimpson Hughes. Dr. Jimpson Hughes."

The dentist was in his fifties. He was pompous and well fed, and a gold watch chain crossed his vest heavily. He puffed to the stand, was sworn. Wentworth smiled at him, and the dentist smiled back.

"Dr. Hughes, did you have a patient named Hanford Tyson?"

"I tended his teeth twenty years," said Dr. Hughes, settling back expansively, "and very complicated work it was, too. He had three pieces of bridgework." He waved his hands. "I kept casts of them, they were so interesting."

Wentworth nodded. "A week ago, Dr. Hughes, you examined a body that was exhumed, a body that had been buried under the name of Hanford Tyson. Will you tell me what you found?"

"It wasn't Tyson."

"You're sure of that?"

"Absolutely. The body was that of a young man, and no dentist has ever touched his teeth. A remarkably fine set of teeth, sir."

"The man who was killed March 12th, buried March 13th, in Tyson's gave, was not Tyson?"

"Absolutely!"

"Do you know where Tyson is now?"

The expansive dentists' head nodded gloomily.

"Where is he?"

"On a slab in the morgue. I examined the teeth yesterday. Tyson is the man who fell in flames from the tower of the Empire State building a week ago."

Wentworth walked away from the dentist, and Glastonbury was after him like a terrier, but failed to shake his story. Finally, he spun toward Wentworth.

"You can't get out of that this easily!" he thundered. "I'll re-indict you for the murder of John Doe, or whoever died in that auto."

"Then," said Wentworth calmly, "it will be brought out that I knew who the man in the auto was, and you'd have to prove a motive for it, and possession of the weapon. In fact," said

Wentworth calmly, "all you can prove is that I was on the scene of the crime."

"I had an affidavit that you stole!" Glastonbury thundered.

Wentworth raised his brows. The Judge leaned forward.

"I'll entertain a motion, Mr. Defense Attorney, to dismiss the indictment."

Glastonbury glowered at Wentworth, then shrugged. "I'll *nolle prosse,*" he stated gloomily. "I also want to *nolle prosse* an indictment against one Nita Van Sloan...."

Wentworth leaned over the bar and shook hands with Glastonbury. "Till we meet again," said Wentworth "I daresay you'll find you've just misplaced those affidavits somewhere or other...."

HE TURNED to Nita, smiling thinly. "That teeth story got Tyson, too. That's what turned the girl on him. I hadn't exhumed the body at that time, hadn't even asked to. But I figured the chief must be Tyson. Because, when the extortion plot was revealed as a fake, the Destroyers *had no reason at all to kill Tucson.*"

They strolled on to a private anteroom off the court room. Wentworth turned to Nita. "Well, jailbird...."

Nita laughed warmly, threw her arms about Wentworth's neck. If it hurt his wounded shoulder, Wentworth said nothing about it. He did not even raise his head when the door opened, didn't look up until Kirkpatrick laid a hand on his shoulder, then he turned to face him, his right arm still about Nita. Kirkpatrick had a suitcase in his hand.

"On the day you were arrested for murder by Glastonbury

and escaped," said Kirkpatrick, "a hatless young man dressed like you went into a rooming house. He carried a suitcase. Out of that house walked one Tito Caliepi, who everyone knows now is the Spider. This suitcase was found in the house, hidden in the chimney of the room where the men found Tito.

"I have had my men trace this suitcase. It was bought by a Hindu... shall I go on?"

Nita's face paled. She forced a laugh and walked toward Kirkpatrick, looked up into his face. If Dick wanted to run....

Wentworth stood fixed, his eyes locked with Kirkpatrick's. It was damning. In itself that suitcase was only a trivial link, but....

"Don't interfere, Nita," said Kirkpatrick quietly. He walked around her and confronted Wentworth. "Dick, you know damned well you're the Spider. I know it, too, and have for a long time."

Wentworth's brows raised slightly. He spread his hands. "Well, if you know it...."

Abruptly Kirkpatrick smiled. "But I can't prove it, Dick. And just between you and me, I rather admire this lad who calls himself the Spider. He gets the crooks I can't reach."

He looked down at the suitcase, frowned sourly.

"The guy who sold this said he couldn't tell one Hindu from another, so this doesn't mean anything." He handed it to Wentworth. "Remember, Dick, if suspicion points to you, if anyone produces evidence against you, I am going through with it to the bitter end. In the meantime, if I can be of any small assistance to you unofficially...."

Kirkpatrick turned and met Nita's eyes. Her face was ludicrous with amazement. Wentworth's mouth was grinning crookedly as he stared down at the suitcase. Kirkpatrick turned in the doorway.

"It's a good thing facial expressions can't be entered as criminal evidence," he said softly, then laughed. The door closed behind him.

Nita raised tear-wet eyes to Wentworth's. She ran to his arms. "Dick, oh, Dick…" she said.

POPULAR PUBLICATIONS
HERO PULPS

LOOK FOR MORE SOON!

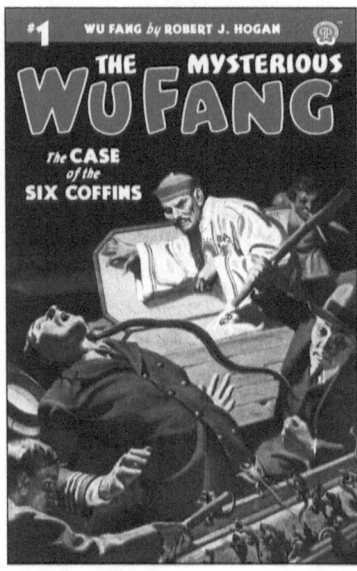

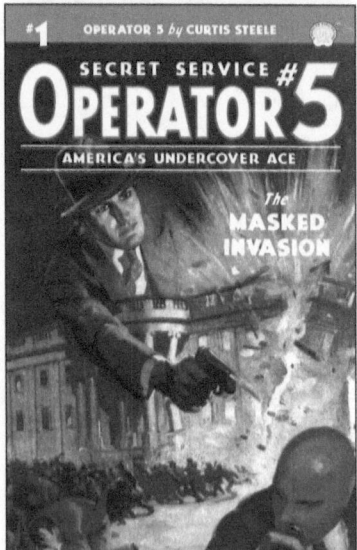

www.ingramcontent.com/pod-product-compliance
Lightning Source LLC
Chambersburg PA
CBHW020425180626
46812CB00003B/1152